Lazy Fascist Review

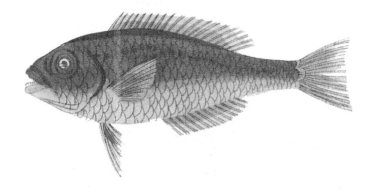

No. 3
August 2015

LAZY FASCIST REVIEW NO. 3

Editor-in-Chief
Cameron Pierce

Editorial Assistant
Bianca Flores

Cover Design
Matthew Revert

ISBN: 978-1-62105-184-8

Lazy Fascist Review is published twice a year
by Lazy Fascist Press, an imprint of Eraserhead Press.

For more information, visit lazyfascistpress.com
or email lazyfascistreview@gmail.com.

PO Box 10065
Portland, OR 97296

Printed in the USA.

CONTENTS

EDITOR'S NOTE
Cameron Pierce

Welcome to the third issue of *Lazy Fascist Review*. When the previous issue was released, my wife and I were moving from Portland to Astoria, a small town on the Oregon coast. We're loving it out here in Astoria. We've been fixing up our World War II era home and caring for our beautiful young daughter, who turned four months old yesterday. Earlier this year, we spent six weeks in Grahamstown, South Africa, where I had the incredible privelege and honor of being a Mellon writer-in-residence at Rhodes University. I was exposed to the work of many brilliant writers in South Africa, including Tania Terblanche, who makes her U.S. debut in this issue with two stories. I hope to see many more stories by her in the future. If you want to check out more work by contemporary South African writers, I recommend *Head On Fire* by Lesego Rampolokeng and *Because the Night* by Stacey Hardy. They're among my favorite books I've read this year and would be right at home in the Lazy Fascist catalog.

In addition to killer stories by Tania Terblanche, Daphne Gottlieb, Allison Floyd, Tiffany Scandal, and Nick Mamatas, this issue features the tour diary of Witch Mountain drummer Nathan Carson, who gives us an inside look at life on the road during their North American tour in support of *Mobile of Angels*, one of the most popular metal albums of 2014. Ever wonder about the realities of a touring doom metal band? Now you'll know. We've also got an interview with Laird Barron, one of the greatest modern authors of weird fiction. And as a final farewell to my old town, this issue features beer pairings and reviews from Portland's Cascade Brewing, maker of fine sour beers. I hope you enjoy *Lazy Fascist Review #3*.

BEARNESS
Tania Terblanche

Recommended Pairing: **Cascade Noyaux**

When you were a brown bear you reared at me on the shore. So much food from the salmon run—your snout glittered with scales. I brought my wading suit and filled it with fish in your wake. You didn't eat anything during your hibernation—your belly swayed from side to side as you dug your den in the ground. I guarded against poachers outside. They brought bear traps. I said there were no bears here. They said they'd leave the bear traps just in case. I carried them around my neck until spring. You were grumpy when you awoke. You dragged your paws and stepped on a rusted nail in the forest.

When you were a panda bear your eyes had black circles

around them. You had me believe that you were sad and fatigued, but it was only the nature of your pelt. I brought my rain coat for the monsoon. My hands were raw from foraging for the bamboo that I brought you. You roared at me in Mandarin and bit my hands when I fed you. When a tiger attacked me you said that you were a herbivore and a pacifist and that you didn't have any teeth. You were pink and patchy from where I clutched at your fur as I got dragged away.

When you were a black bear you had a white crescent moon on your chest. I brought my suction cup suit to climb up to you. You were eating the moths that were as confused as I was about the idea of two moons. You stepped on my head when you climbed down and said that you had a stomach ache. I said that it was your own fault for eating wood and termites at the same time. I rubbed your belly until you fell asleep with your long claws tucked under your head for a while.

When you were a sun bear your skin was hard and coarse. We were living in the forest for too long and it was quiet because there were spider webs in my ears. Your long pink tongue pulled out the spiders from inside, leaving the droplets of your saliva to drip incessantly onto my eardrums. I brought my bee suit and watched you break apart a hive with a ribcage crack. Your jaws chomped down onto vibrating bees. I joined in your feast, as I had also learned to search for a small bit of sweetness beneath the stings.

When you were a polar bear your fur was tinged copper

with blood. I dove to watch the seals make jet lines around you in the black waters, like bobbing grey balloons. When you swam away from me and the next ice cap was too far for you to reach, the shore a distant plateau with waves lapping from the ripples you sent long ago, I steamed up my goggles with my warm breath so that your flailing bear paws in the current made it seem as if you were waving.

I hiked back to my tent that had been whipped by arctic winds. I climbed into it and tore my wet suit at the seams.

When you were nothing but a bear suit, the two of us slept on the saline damp of your bareness spread over the bed.

THE INTIMATE MUSEUM OF ABSENCE
Daphne Gottlieb

Recommended Pairing: **Cascade Sang Royal**

When she asked me to accompany her to the Intimate Museum of Absence, I said *Sure, I love museums.*

She said *Great*, and gave me the address. It was her apartment.

At the front door, she rushed me in, excited, kissing my cheek. She took my hand—hers was warm, soft—and led me down the long, dark hall to her bedroom door. *Stay still,* she said. She meant it. She pulled out a pocketknife and sliced off the left point of the collar on my shirt. I liked that shirt. It was a nice one, dark blue.

There was a big glass jar by the door. Inside were scraps of fabric, pieces of hair, and one or two pieces of silver jewelry.

She fed the scrap of my collar into the jar. It was a hungry jar. She had serious eyes. *Admission*, she said. *One-time only. Your collar is your receipt.* I nodded.

Her room was small, chaotic. In the middle of her room was her neatly made bed. In the middle of her bed, a small black kitten devotedly kneaded a blanket the color of the sky. *Welcome to the Intimate Museum of Absence*, she said, spreading her arms solemnly and pushing the door back farther, revealing a wall crammed floor-to-ceiling with things. *Would you like a guided tour?* she asked, arching an eyebrow. There was barely room to walk in her thicket of things. A plant covered the room. Up the walls. Across the ceiling. The plant owned everything. It had everything in the room in its grasp—it held things in tendrils and in curls, in chokeholds and coils. If it was in the room, it belonged to the plant. I figured, she owned the plant. She was in good. I figured, that meant good things for my survival rate. *Sure*, I said. *I think a docent is a great idea.*

She shifted her weight a few times from left to right and cleared her throat before planting her feet heavily and declaring, arms spread again what little they could, *Welcome to the Intimate Museum of Absence. I am pleased to be your guide today. Here, to your left, you will notice our fine Things in Jars collection. In the jar that looks like it's full of snot, you will see a jellyfish. In the jar that looks like it's full of feces, there is a sea cucumber. These,* she said, gesturing to the row of jars above the row of jars, *are brittle stars. There are five because you can never have too many brittle stars in the bedroom. And here,* she said, pushing a leaf aside above the jars to reveal a small shrine made of the skulls of what looked like small mammals, *we have a fetal mouse. We call him "The King."*

I nodded. *Why do you call him "The King"?* I asked. It seemed a very funny name for such a small, hairless, bubblegum-colored rodent.

She looked at me and smiled indulgently, very softly, *Because he's The King!* She moved her hand and a leaf fell in front of the tiny ossuary again with a gentle sweeping noise. The small black cat continued to knead the pillow, as if it was generating whatever was needed to power the museum, as if the planet depended on the cat's kneading to rotate.

Ready to move on? she asked. She knocked on a shockingly peach-colored wooden leg, *Here, we have a wooden leg.* The leg was wearing a shoe. There was a sock pulled up calf-high. Under the sock, there were white bandages and tape. She reached down to the floor next to the leg and struggled with the plant until she was able to free a pair of small boots. The boots were made of buckles and laces, it seemed, with metal hinges up one side. The toes were open. I touched the small open toe of one, as I wondered what sort of child would wear shoes like these. *Polio braces,* she said. She looked like she was thinking. *You wear glasses,* she said. I took my fingers out of the shoe. *Yes. I have since I was four,* I said. She put the shoe on the floor, shoving vines aside with her hand, careful not to let the shoes rest on any part of the plant. Then she slid her own shoes off, and lined them up right next to the tiny leg cages.

Thank you for coming to the Intimate Museum of Absence, she said with an inappropriate enthusiasm. *Do you have any questions?*

I had many. I didn't know where to start. *This is a supreme collection,* I started, falteringly, *and I'm very impressed with the range and depth of your museum.* She had a birthday smile on. She was ready to open the gift. *I guess what I'm saying is*—she cocked her head expectantly. My neck was warm. *Well, I like everything in here, but I don't really understand why you call it the "Intimate Museum of Absence" when everything here is, well, here.*

Her eyes lit up like she had swallowed the harvest moon. I looked back and the kitten was once again milking the pillow determinedly. *Everything here is absent something else,* she said. *The wooden leg is absent the body that gave it a purpose. The braces are absent the child. Everything in here is whole, an object unto itself. It's not partial. But its existence speaks of the absence of what made it valuable.*

The moon turned golden and almost shimmered.

What about the kitten, I asked.

She's on break right now, she said. I looked over. She was right. The kitten was fast asleep, a comma on the pillow.

The doll limbs must be absent their dolls, I thought, reaching my hand out to touch plastic fingertips. The fingertips connected to the fingers, which were connected to the rest of the doll hidden in the plant. *The dolls?* I asked, surprised.

The dolls are absent the girls who love them.

And the plant?

She laughed. *It is absent the jungle. I think that is why this plant holds on to everything it touches. It doesn't want to be alone again.*

She reached up and fingered my cut place, the spot on my collar that her knife had kissed. Our mouths met like the sides of a wound newly meeting again. Something torn apart was being repaired. Or something. The twilight closed up around our touch. Sometime before the grayblue became blueblack, the kitten woke up and started purring. I took off my glasses. In the faded light, we counted each other's scars.

GARBAGE HEART
Allison Floyd

Recommended Pairing: **Cascade Strawberry**

Muriel had a garbage heart, and that was good for two things: compost and burn piles. She figured if she couldn't grow things there, she could set them on fire. Like most things, her garbage heart was congenital. She tried not to let it get her down. After all, she thought, if you could grow porcinis atop dung piles, you could make do with a garbage heart.

One day she decided to place a personal ad on a popular online dating site:

Girl with a garbage heart seeks fertile ground or fuel. Not sure which. Help me disambiguate!

This was one of those "alternative lifestyle" sites. Muriel didn't lead an alternative lifestyle, but she figured the site was her best bet since garbage hearts were out of the mainstream.

A day passed. The responses didn't come pouring in.

A week passed. Compulsive clicks of the "Refresh" button did nothing to alleviate the barrenness of Muriel's inbox.

Another week passed. Tumbleweeds.

And then: a lone email. Its Subject line: Take Out the Garbage.

His screen name was Garbage Man. His profile consisted of a single line: Cleanliness is Next to Godliness.

Muriel and the Garbage Man exchanged emails and eventually phone numbers.

"I'm intrigued by you," she said during their first phone call. "But my concern is that we don't have much in common. I have a garbage heart and you have this preoccupation with cleanliness."

"Opposites attract," the Garbage Man said.

They met for a picnic at a landfill. The Garbage Man wore latex gloves. Muriel laid her garbage heart bare for him. She hadn't been on many dates and she thought this was what you were supposed to do. The Garbage Man emptied the picnic basket and removed a collection of cleaning supplies: bleach, steel wool, and white vinegar.

"I'm going to give you a scouring you'll never forget," he said.

And he did.

They continued to see each other. Muriel had to admit it was nice to be clean. The Garbage Man took a mop to the viscous puddles of her insides, wiped her grimy surfaces from top to bottom, raided the drawers of her soul's refrigerator, and tossed everything that had gone bad, which didn't leave much.

Yes, it was nice to be clean, but something was missing.

"Don't get me wrong," she told him. "I appreciate everything you've done. But I want to grow things, or burn them. I want my heart to have something to show for itself."

"Your heart has me," the Garbage Man said.

She decided to plant an herb garden in the backyard. She scooped the contraband coffee grinds, eggshells, and rotten vegetables she'd stowed in an old coffee can she hid in her left ventricle and released them into the patch of soil she'd designated. She planted rows of basil, mint, parsley, chives, cilantro, rosemary, and dill. After a week or two the incipient green sprouts reared their heads.

Muriel surveyed the soil with satisfaction. At last, she thought, my heart has something to show for itself: something all my own. To celebrate, she went inside and wallowed in the secret slop—since she was with the Garbage Man, she had to keep the slop secret now—of her garbage heart.

When the Garbage Man returned to the home they now shared, he took one look at her and frowned. She seemed even messier than usual somehow.

The next morning Muriel headed to the backyard, holding a mug of coffee. She savored the pleasurable anticipation of checking on the herb garden. Her herb garden. As she stepped off the porch and glanced toward the corner where the herb garden was, the mug slipped from her fingers, spewing its contents onto the ground. Muriel felt the scalding coffee droplets splatter her feet, but she didn't care. She ran to the corner and halted, staring dumbfounded at the ground. It was gone. Her herb garden was gone. The rows had been flattened and covered with a series of pristine cinderblocks arranged in the shape of a heart.

Muriel stared at the cinderblocks for a long time.

The Garbage Man approached Muriel from behind and placed his hands on her shoulders, breaking her trance.

She shrugged his hands off her shoulders. "What happened?"

His hands found her shoulders again and tightened their grip. "It was a mess. There was dirt everywhere. I had to fix it. These blocks will be easy to keep clean. We can just hose them down when we need to."

Muriel knew in this moment the answer to her heart's original question about compost versus fuel. She wrested herself from the Garbage Man's grip and headed inside.

He looked at the ground and frowned. "You spilled your coffee."

Oh, Muriel thought, I'll spill more than that.

She retrieved the matches from the kitchen drawer and a can of gasoline from the garage. She heard the kitchen door close behind the Garbage Man. He was carrying the coffee mug she had dropped.

"You should be more careful," he said.

She coaxed her face into a smile. "Moot point."

It was then that he took note of the can of gasoline in her hands. As she did, she opened it and doused them both, and the kitchen floor. Before the Garbage Man had fully registered what she was doing—what a mess she was making!—she lit a match and tossed it on the ground. He felt his mouth contort into a rictus. He'd gotten what he wanted, but it wasn't what he thought it would be. He knew when he met her that she was incendiary, and cleanliness was next to godliness, and nothing cleansed like fire. And no one needed cleansing more than he did. But somehow the burn lacked the heat he had hoped for.

Muriel, for her part, thought the same thing.

BUNDLES
Tania Terblanche

Recommended Pairing: **Cascade Gose**

My friends bring me over in summer mostly, so that I can divert the mosquitoes. They breed in the back garden, where there is a brackish pond that the dog no longer drinks from. My friends can't stand the itching that bubbles up from their skin in yellowish welts and they reward me to endure it on their behalf by doing my washing all summer, which I bring to them in bundles.

My friends have a top of the line washing machine. They brought it home last summer, swaddled in polystyrene, from a sterile room with lots of reflective surfaces. It's been whirring ever since—always full but never finished. I sweat a lot around my friends. I don't get to visit the aquariums in summer, but I am content to sit on the cool floor and watch my sheets swirl by, floating past like foaming jellyfish when one or another cycle of the washing machine is complete and brings the world to a ghostly halt.

Mosquitoes really like my blood because it's a sort of cocktail. I had a blood transfusion once because of tick fever that I noticed too late. My friends' sheep dog is always digging in the garden, among the long grass that grows wildly near the pond and she shares a bed with me—a small bed in a separate room that my friends never finished painting.

My friends say what a relief that I'm here now—that they have their hands full and can't waste any more time on scratching. The husband has a bundle wrapped in a blanket that he's rocking in his arms. His wife has a bundle strapped to her chest. I lift its folds to find a silver cutlery set still in its packaging. I stroke her belly, where she has stuffed a feather pillow in under her dress.

The television wails and the husband says it's his turn. He shuffles off, pushing his bundle into my arms. I unwrap it to find a computer game inside. The husband watches over the television until it quiets down.

*

The wife and I sit on old chairs in the back garden. They're covered in canvas, for the sun and rain, she says. They creak from our weight. The wife props her feet up on my lap and I rub them because she says they're swollen. A mosquito hovers over her ankle, before deciding to settle on my wrist.

Mosquitoes really like my blood because it's a sort of shooter. My mother and father's blood never quite took inside me. It floats around my veins in oily layers that don't have the same density. The mosquitoes pull up their bar chairs and pass out drunk around my ankles and my feet, where the veins fork closest to the surface.

The sheep dog cuts through the grass, rustling it with her black tail sticking out like a shark fin. I lift the wife's legs, her ankles in my palm, and scratch at my neck with my free hand. I want to know what's in the garden where the dog digs. She says there are only more mosquitoes and tells me that it's time to wash my shirt.

It sticks to my stomach when I take it off. The wife gathers a fresh bundle of clothes and sings to it while I undress in the wash room. She hands the bundle to me and flops the sweat-drenched heap into the washing machine. The buttons of my trousers bang against the dark inner lining of the machine—thrusting with hollow metal echoes.

*

My friends are exhausted by the late afternoon. They spend all morning gathering the right things into the right bundles and carrying them around the house until they are old enough to find their rightful place. I fix us an early dinner of cool summer fruits and leaves, with meats cut into thin films. My friends sit listlessly at the table, each of them fingering a bundle or hopping one up and down on their knees.

By the time we are finished eating, my friends barely have any strength left and I carry the wife to their bed. I come back for the husband and wrap his massive arms around my neck for him to lean on me on his way to her.

The husband jerks the pillow out from under his wife's dress and hugs it tightly to his chest. They prop a bundle of duvet up between them and fall into a deep sleep.

I sit on my small bed and scratch. I want to sleep through the twilight as well, through the mosquitoes' most active time. I wait for the sheep dog to join me, but she doesn't come and I go looking for her in the house. I find her herding the bundles into corners. My friends leave them lying all over the house. The sheep dog runs them up drawers and tables and they scurry into cabinets. She plays tug of war with their wrappings and spins them out of their blankets. When all of them are in their rightful places, she lies panting on the floor. The bundles, too, seem to breathe a bit before they start gathering dust.

*

At the peak of summer I become anemic. My skin breaks out in hives from the bumps of baby mosquito bites at which I scratch my nails into a pulp. There are big mosquitoes too that drift over to me lazily and like pesticide aircrafts they swiftly deposit their saliva into me before I can even feel them on my skin. My blood is their fuel. They park themselves on my ceiling and wait poised until I turn the lights out every night. I listen to the sound of their wings in the dark—the voodoo violins that they play for me in secret, for my ears only.

Mosquitoes really like my blood because it's sort of easy to reach. My skin is soft and thin, my pores are generous. I don't have a lot of hair on my body and I breathe deeply and sweetly. The sheep dog lies at my feet, occasionally snapping at one of the insects that hover there. We never sleep under the covers in summer.

My friends sleep undisturbed. They take a nap at dusk and dress themselves in cool white pajamas before going to bed at midnight, when they fall into a comatose sleep that is interrupted only by their bedside radio at dawn. It screeches at them to change its frequency before they go about their daily bundling.

I can't seem to get any sleep anymore. Every evening after I have carried my friends to bed and the sheep dog has finished herding the bundles through the house, she looks up at me with her uncanny brown eyes and tries to herd me through the back door, into the garden. At the peak of summer I no longer have the strength to outsmart her or to fight her and one day I let her lead me into the grass. Like a koi fish lazily passing a lotus in a pond she sweeps me along, cutting a path through grass as tall as my shoulders.

We end up in a clearing where the blue light of dusk seems to be thicker and where several piles of small stones lie heaped on the ground. I look back to the house, which seems further now than I could have imagined.

A thin trail of smoke drifts up from one of the piles and I see the wife perched on top of the heap, a long cigarette holder between her fingers. She glares at me from behind giant round sunglasses that cover all of her temples and her eyebrows. She taps at the holder to let a clump of ash fall down and in between the stones. Her legs are spindly in striped stockings—splayed atop the pile at impossible angles.

The dog settles down at my feet, making herself small and flat behind me. The whites of her eyes glisten in the increasing darkness. She is silent except for the occasional whimper—the inverted whistling sound of sheep dogs. When the coal from the cigarette lights up the wife's face with every drag, I can see its embers reflected in each of her dozens of eyes as they try to decipher me behind the glasses. It isn't the wife after all.

Her cigarette is finished and she removes it from its holder, taking care to stomp it out completely with her heel, before crouching in front of the pile of stones. She plants her cigarette holder in the middle of the stones and closes her lips around it more tightly than before. The woman who is not the wife does not let go of my gaze while she sucks at something that is buried underneath the bundle of stones, her makeshift straw pulsating.

*

The sheep dog follows me everywhere, supporting me when I stumble and licking my face when I pass out on the floor in front of the washing machine. I am happy that my friends' skins are smooth once again and that their strength has returned.

They maneuver through the house in increasingly animated ways every day, bundling their treasures and taking care of them. The husband brings me a bowl of fruit at noon, saying that I look too pale and that the sugar will make me feel better. He drinks the juices from his own bowl, which he balances on one palm while he cradles a wrapped electric razor in his free arm. To his back he has fastened a rolled-up bedspread and when I ask if we are going camping he laughs and squeezes my shoulder really hard.

The wife passes me in the hallway and lets her fingers run across the small of my back to feel how much I am sweating. Her nails are long and tingling. They slide across the bumps and scabs on my spine. The itching returns when she lets go, even worse than before. I grope at her belly where this time she has stuffed a teddy bear in under her blouse. Its price tag dangles over her belly button. Its eyes are black pearls under the white of the fabric, of her skin.

She stays with me until past midnight, on the cool floor of the wash room, lying flat on her back and resting her feet against my chest. I nestle my head between her knees and wait for her breathing to become soft and even before I pry a small bundle of earrings from her fingers and carry her to the husband who is curled up in their bed.

I watch over the sheep dog as she herds the bundles. She barks and plays, her paws scuttling across the tiles, her ears flopping happily. She rushes from one room to the next, tongue trailing behind her. Her human brown eyes smile at me for approval. She brings me a package covered in bubble-wrap from which I tear the tape for her. She chews at it until the vase inside is exposed. It rolls towards an open cupboard and comes to rest. It is only when the back door opens that the dog gives a suspended inwards whistle and slowly backs into a corner.

The woman who is not the wife walks into the wash room, her striped legs blurry in the fluorescent light. She sweeps through the kitchen and towards us. The lights are reflected a hundred times in the eyes behind her glasses, but she does not seem to be looking at us. Strapped to her back is a cart that is formed like an abdomen—bean-shaped, bulging and shiny, trailing behind her on the tiniest of wheels. She takes care to maneuver it through the doorways and into the living room, where scattered bundles of treasures still lie, waiting to be herded into their rightful places.

The dog and I watch in silence as the woman gathers the bundles and deposits them into her cart. Slowly she picks each bundle up from the floor, poking at the folds with her cigarette holder to see what's inside and then closing it up again by twirling the fabric over the opening. She moves silently, the only sound a faint creaking from the wheels of the cart under the weight of the packages.

By the time she gets to the hallway leading to the bedrooms her cart is full. She stands there for a moment, palms resting against the opposite walls of the narrow corridor, elbows jutting out at the side. She seems to be listening, to be smelling. But she soon reverses, walking backwards with her cart until she is out in the open once more, where she can turn around and proceed to the kitchen and through the wash room out the back door.

The sheep dog and I watch through the dining room windows as she stops at the pond, where she crouches down. The woman who is not the wife blows bubbles in the brackish water with her cigarette holder, before lighting a cigarette and making her way back through the grass. The ribbon of smoke and the wheel prints on the ground stay behind in her wake before they, too, dissipate as though they had never been there.

*

My friends do not miss their bundles that disappear from the house every night. They seem to have a source of unlimited new bundles, or perhaps they recycle older ones, but as far as I know my friends never revisit the treasures that they once nursed with the greatest care. They seem to be fixated on the new, the unopened.

Either way, I decide not to tell my friends about the disappearance of their bundles, keeping it buried inside me as much as the urge to scratch at my body, which is a field of sores that re-open every time I lose control for a moment and dig up the itch that I managed to keep stifled for a while.

My friends start looking at me worriedly, lifting up my shirt to check the severity of my mosquito bites. The wife washes my clothes more frequently and I try my best to keep my secrets from her especially. She wraps bandages around my middle, where the mosquitoes have bitten through my thinning shirt, and she dabs at me with salves that stop the itching for a while and seep into my pores with minty coolness.

When the woman hauls her cart into the house at night, I try to ignore her by busying myself with dusting off the treasures that lie buried in drawers and displayed on stands around the house. On one such a night I discover something in the television rack, a large parcel wrapped in cloth and tied with string, resting among wires from various electronic controllers and charging cables.

Inside the bundle I find a candle as large as a water bucket. It is yellow too and smells of the forest—citronella, the kind that repels insects. I light it with my swollen fingers, slightly searing the bandages around my hands. I fall asleep next to the lit candle, waking up when it is light outside, with blurry vision underneath swollen eyelids that were, up to now, free of any mosquito bites.

*

I spend my days on my small bed in the separate room where the sheep dog lies in the doorway. I wrap my arms around my candle and breathe through my mouth. I am woken only by the fingers of the wife changing my bandages and trying to lift me so she can get a fresh shirt on me. This happens so frequently that I imagine she leaves me lying naked and sweating on the bed after a while, closing the door behind her.

When night falls I hear the faint screeching of wheels on the tiles and reach out my hand to the dog to calm her whistling. The cart comes ever closer through the hallway, its wheels jerking over the cracks in the tiles, stabilizing again to press forward. I crawl out of bed and drape myself across the hallway, in front of the door to the small room with its peeling paint.

I light my candle and look up to the woman. Its tall flame licks at her glasses, reflected in the eyes beneath. She puts her cigarette holder between her lips and pinches her nose. She retraces her steps, backwards through the hallway, pushing the cart with her back until she is out of sight and in the living room once again. The woman who is not the wife continues to forage for treasures, her shadow long and spindly in the light of the candle, the only light now in the house.

I feel the hands of the wife wrap me in a blanket, swaddling me like a larva and trying several times to pick me up. She carries me to their bedroom, where she places me on the bed. With me wedged between them, a soft solid bundle, I fall into a feverish sleep as my friends watch the shadows of what was once important to them dance against the walls.

THE READING
Tiffany Scandal

Recommended Pairing: **Oblique B&W Coffee Stout**

Just look at them.

They're sitting around the distressed-wood table on salvaged school chairs, wearing the finest in hobo-chic fashion. You've seen it before. This is that kind of city. I can't help but see them stand out at the center of the room, painfully cool, talking over the black coffees set uniformly in front of them, more of an accessory than a stimulant. The sunset's casting like a stage light, and from a certain angle, their silhouettes against the wall are statues while shadows of limbs dance and flail on the floor. They look like demons.

The one nearest to me, "Bunny," is wearing his hair in a greasy man bun. His beard is the kind with a sculpted handlebar that went out of fashion three years ago.

Reflective Ray-Bans hide his eyes. When it's not his turn to speak, he pets the rabbit tattooed at the base of his thumb on his left hand.

Clockwise:

"Umi" has long, cherry hair and thick, black-framed glasses that aren't prescriptive, because *who cares, it's fashion.* The purse on the table beside her looks like a giant egg and is bigger than her head, like a fancy shoplifter bag. She keeps a firm grip on its handle like whatever's inside might try to get out or she's ready to use it for self-defense.

"Rachel" is the one that looks like she belongs in a '90s sitcom, stringy blonde hair and a waifish frame. Terrible posture. It's hard to tell if she's too small or the clothes she's wearing are too big. I didn't see her standing up. You can see the bags under her eyes from here, like she spends more nights crying than she does sleeping. Must've recently broken up with her artist girlfriend.

"Nelson," the blue-eyed albino, is the quiet one. There isn't much to consider about him, except that even as the sky darkens, the light coming in makes his skin glow like it's just about to catch fire. That'd be something…

The espresso machine whirs. Heavy coffee aroma in the air. Grounds on the ground. Shoes need coffee, too.

Bunny is a trust-fund baby. His whims prepaid by mommy and daddy because all he's got to do is carry on the family name. He spends much of his time looking from windows, watching a world pass him by. He sometimes volunteers at homeless shelters downtown, but folks there don't like to talk to him because though they don't know wealth, they understand its stink. He writes shitty poems on his iPhone and reads them to whoever will listen, or happens to be nearby. His favorite color is taupe.

Umi works at Buffalo Exchange. As a child, she competed in beauty pageants. She was a cheerleader until junior high, when she discovered The Used and felt the lyrics really spoke to her, and she started smoking pot and kissing girls, and wearing only pink and black. Now she listens to hip-hop and identifies as a feminist but takes a passive role in her relationships with men. Her parents don't understand her, but they hope it's a phase—and it is. They're still waiting for the phone call that'll tell them she's gotten her life together.

Rachel...oh, Rachel. She moved here from Connecticut. Heard the art scene in Portland was booming and moved here to be in the middle of it, despite the fact that she has no talent. An introvert trying to break out of her shell. She's a hanger-on. But social situations make her nervous and she picks at her scalp, and at scabs from other times she's picked at it. Small dogs frighten her.

Nelson might not be talkative, but it's only because he doesn't like any of the people he's with. He's obsessed with selfies and pictures of empty plates, and excessive hashtagging. He doesn't tip. He writes his name in block letters and surrounds it with doodles on the bill. He dates a new woman every week, half-listening and smirking at imagined ways the potential will give up their dignity. He refers to these women as "strumpets." As soon as he gets what he wants, he's gone. He sometimes thinks about calling up old dates, putting together a Harem. He's sure he could get a few girls to come back. Because, you know, he's *that* good. At least, that's what he would like to believe.

Bunny pets the rabbit on his hand, watches Rachel.

"You got out."

"Yeah." Umi, cocking her head to the side, smiles.

Bunny shoots a startled glance at Umi, like he's just noticed she's sitting there.

"What was it like?" Rachel brings her knees to her chest and traces the designs on her shoes.

"What?"

Rachel says "Jail" like it's something romantic.

"It was okay, I guess. I wasn't there long."

"What'd you even do, again?"

"Oh, I tried to burn down Tim's house. I think he's going to drop the charges, though." Umi nodding along.

"How you figure that?" says Bunny. He inches sideways on his chair, away from Umi. Maybe he's scared of her— they used to date, and he's still seeing a therapist to work out the trauma of their two weeks together.

"He sent a text asking how's it going, and invited me to dinner."

Everyone at the table nods in a way that says they don't know how not to encourage her when she gets bad ideas. She's got the ring on her left hand. . . After they broke it off, Umi stalked her ex for a week—sitting in her car down the street from his house, crying for the helplessness and anger, wiping snot and tears on her sleeve, a panting sound that's both a growl and a whimper. Umi finally decided to take action after watching him bring home woman after woman. Scaled the side of his house and banged on the bedroom window, and tried to set fire to the curtains for emphasis on why he needed to take her back. The cops were called and as they're taking her away in cuffs, he gets a good look at her and realizes that's the crazy he needs in his life. Now they're planning on getting married next month.

The story's interrupted by a bullhorn. Bunny reaches into his pocket for a flip phone that looks like it barely survived its journey from the year 2004. He silences it and sets it on the table. Another thing he does in his free time is sell drugs. He doesn't need the money, rather, the idea of getting caught excites him. Hence the burner's abrasive ringtone.

Nelson is watching Umi from his place across the table. Tearing her apart in his head. He's jealous, he's been in love with her since they met, but she hasn't given him so much as a signal. Even now, she doesn't even look him in the eye. Speaks casually when referencing him like he's not even there. She laughs; he looks down.

Rachel slides her hand across the table and gently touches his wrist. Without looking up, he smiles, pursed. The constant rejection from Umi hurts more than anything else, than any other pain he's been through. More than the Christmas where…

"Doug, how are you holding up?"

Nelson shrugs—wait, did she say Doug? Okay, okay. That changes his story slightly.

Bunny and Umi both lean in, seeming concerned.

"Can we see?"

The albino opens his mouth and reveals an uneven stump where his tongue was. You can see the others trying their best to be polite. But they can't help it, can they? The morbid fascination that something like this happened to one of their own… How long until it becomes fashion? Bunny shakes his head. Rachel is looking into his mouth like it's at the end of a long hallway. Umi is squinting, then widening her eyes, then squinting, and so on. She does this for a very long time. At least it feels that way.

So maybe "Doug" witnessed a murder and was forced into silence.

"I really thought the seizure thing was a myth," says Umi. "You know, like Pop Rocks and Coke."

Oh, he's epileptic?

"I remember this time that—"

"Did one of you order a sandwich?" They're interrupted by one of the baristas, a young blonde girl, carrying a plate.

"No, I don't think so."

"Nope."

"Not me."

" … "

Everyone at the table shaking their head. The barista walks away.

"So one time—"

"Hey Bree, so are Tim and your mom still planning to sell their house?"

Bunny's been cut off for the second time. His lips purse, just staring at Rachel. He prods the rabbit on his left hand like it's done something wrong. I bet this happens to him often when he's around them, especially now that Albino Doug's become so speechless. I wonder how long they've known each other. They seem thick as thieves. Maybe it's the division of privilege—Bunny doesn't get to finish because he's a man, but Doug's exempt because he has no voice.

"What?" says Umi, err, "Bree."

"I asked if your mom was still going to sell the house?"

Why the mention of this "Tim" separately and not the second time? Easy. Bree was having an affair with her mother's second husband and they got caught. As repentance, Tim offered to pack up and leave to create a fresh start with her, away from Bree. They're going to sell the house Bree's father built so they can live on a boat. Just them. Bree's been cut from the inheritance.

"They've got to, yeah. Her boyfriend hasn't been able to find work and the unemployment's just about run out. She's on disability, but it's not enough for the mortgage payments. If it doesn't sell soon, the bank's going to eat it."

Okay, so he lost his job because he couldn't focus on his work while they were having the affair. Her mother's only on disability because they got into a fight over him and Bree pushed her down some stairs. She's in a wheelchair, now.

"Rough."

"So, like, why exactly were you trying to burn it down?" Rachel still picking at her scalp. Really digging her nails in there. I'm almost expecting blood to come dripping down her forehead soon.

"I was really angry. It felt like he was focusing too much on selling our house instead of worrying about mom. The car accident changed everything. It took a lot from us. I figured if I could get him to stop thinking about money, maybe he'd realize how difficult this has been for her. Dad bought the thing—it's not like Tim has any claim to it."

"And you actually tried to burn it down?"

"Well, I pretty much threatened to. I made a bit of scene. I just got so fucking pissed and some shit got broke. I started screaming and tried to fight Tim. Scratched his face pretty good. The neighbors heard us and called the cops. It didn't help that I was drinking. I'm not exactly proud of it. We've talked since. I think things will be better. Tim's actually a good guy, I realize that, it's just…ah, never mind." Bree rubs Bunny's shoulder. "Were you trying to say something earlier, honey?"

Bunny smiles. The moment's passed. He's not going to say anything because it's apparent that they don't care what he has to say.

"Yeah, nothing important. It was just, when I was, like, seventeen, I saw this guy bite a chunk of his tongue off at a Bikini Kill show. Not to take away from Doug. . ."

Rachel's nose is bleeding.

Bree says, "Bikini Kill...that's the one with—?"

"Kathleen Hanna."

"Yeah. I *love* her. Did you see *The Punk Singer*? That shit changed my life."

...

Rachel holds a napkin under her nostrils and holds her head back.

"You okay?"

Rachel nods.

"You're not supposed to lean your head back. Tuck your head into your chin that way you don't swallow your own blood."

"Like this?" Rachel lurches her chin forward. Another spurt of blood comes out of her nose.

Doug gets up from his chair and moves her chin down. She looks up at him and smiles. He pats her back and goes back to her seat.

Okay, well, Bunny is still a trust fund kid and Rachel's from...

"Connecticut? Like, where the fuck is that, even? That's in New York, right?"

"Close to New York." Bunny is flicking the tattoo now.

"You ever been?"

Bunny nods. "A friend of mine got into Yale and I helped him move in. We packed his stuff into my station wagon and made the drive. From Brooklyn, where we were living. This was before it was all MacBooks and art students. I think seeing Yale was the closest I've ever felt to being rich."

"I love Brooklyn!" Bree staring into her coffee, dreamily. They still haven't had any.

Bree seems the type that loves everything, no matter what.

"It was such a cool place before it got all gentrified, just like what they're doing here."

"You know how I feel about that."

One of Bunny's eyebrows arches over his Ray-Bans.

"Gentrification kills culture to promote tourism. Then what's the point? The culture is the draw in the first place."

"They've been trying to fuck up New Orleans, too, since Katrina."

"Developers are fucking vampires, man."

Yet despite this they're all sitting in the middle of one of the most trendy coffee roasting establishments in town.

"You ever feel like it's our fault? Like we cause this, moving here?"

Doug writes something on a piece of paper and shows it to the group. I imagine that it says "Why are we here?" Because becoming a kind of mute has given him a wisdom beyond his years. But he doesn't mean the coffee shop, nor the city, he means life. He's in an existential crisis born from the solitude of his inability to communicate. You can hear Bunny going "Hmm" this far away.

Rachel goes slack-jawed again. Doug nudges her arm and points to his mouth like he's letting her know she's doing that thing again. She straightens up and closes her mouth.

"Anyone want to go to Powell's?"

"Sure."

Doug shrugs and drops a ten on the table.

Then they're gone.

A young woman walks in after them. Low cut top revealing firm, natural cleavage. Tattoos everywhere. Looks like she works out—maybe CrossFit or she's a dancer. The woman sits at a small table by the windows and orders a cappuccino. The coffee shop's closing soon. She sets out a stack of papers and envelopes and starts counting small bills. Yeah, she's got to be a dancer. She's figuring out finances, monthly expenses, the distribution of her hard-earned money.

One of the baristas walks over to her with the mug. "I think I'm finally getting better at the foam art."

"That looks like a tornado."

"It's a heart. At least, it's supposed to be."

"You'll get there."

The barista nods and starts to walk back to the bar, then stops and looks back at the woman. "Hey boss, where should we put the overstock on the retail delivery?"

"Downstairs, in the dry storage is where it normally goes."

"Oh, okay." The barista perks up and gets back to it. I try to think of a hidden history for her and can't seem to. She's tough to get a line on. When I glance up at the bar a little later, I notice that she's watching me and whispering to a coworker. When they start laughing about something, I can't help but wonder what they're saying, who they think I am. Reading me like I've been reading people. Is this supposed to be a game?

LAB RAT
Nick Mamatas

Recommended Pairing: **Cascade Vlad the Imp Aler**

Occupation: *Freelance.*

—Freelance what?

—Right now, I'm pretty much doing this. Four or five studies a week here at psych, some at the i-lab at the business school. A few at MIT, and one time I did one at Northeastern.

. . .

—Okay, freelance writer. But honestly, I've done so little of it lately I feel like I should just say "freelance" and leave it at that.

—What do you write?

—A little of everything. I have a novel with a small press. I wrote some stuff for the *Phoenix* before they went under.

But I'll do anything: OKCupid profiles for foreign students, brochures and manuals, resumes and cover letters.

—Must be plenty of call for that these days.

—Not as much as you might think. After all, if I were so great at writing cover letters, why I am coming to the Harvard psych lab twice a day to play games and answer questions for ten or twenty bucks a pop?

—Hmm, fair enough. Let me go through the rest of this…

DO THOUGHTS OF HARMING OTHERS, OR YOURSELF, ENTER YOUR MIND DURING THE COURSE OF THE DAY (1-5 scale, 1 being never, 5 being constantly): *4*.

—Four is…high. I have an obligation, uhm, here it is. This is a sheet of resources. You know, phone numbers. Places you can contact if you think you're having some trouble.

—Thanks. I'm fine. You should read my novel.

—I wonder if we have it in the library. I guess you won't get any royalties if I get it from there, right? Haha.

—Eh, it's fine. You buying a copy means that I get one dollar and twelve cents, maybe, eighteen months from now. Basically, whatever money the book is going to make, it's already made.

—All right.

—My novel has a few murders in it. Sort of horror/suspense.

—Okay.

—That's why I put down a 4 for that question. I think about death and murder a lot. For creative reasons.

—Understood. Got it.

—Because I'm a woman, people often think I write

chicklit or something like that.

—Okay, so what we're going to do now is have you place your hand on this block. Then I am going to bring this iron rod over and swing it over like this. See the hinge? Anyway, I'll place it atop the back of your hand. I'm not going to drop it or slam it, just place it, so the point on the bottom will make contact with the exact middle of the back of your hand. It'll start feeling heavier, as the point will sink into the skin of your hand. But it's okay, it won't break the skin or anything like that. You won't get any more, or any less, money if you give up right away or last for a long time. Let me know when the pain becomes unbearable.

—Unbearable? You mean when I can't possibly stand another second of it?

—Well, when you get uncomfortable. Significant discomfort; not just mild. This is all part of what we're trying to measure.

—Am I allowed to talk now, or will that just be a distraction?

—Oh no, we're supposed to talk. I even have talking points, see?

The weather.
Psychology.
Subject's occupation, if any.
Subject's prior experiences with pain and pain management.

—Ha. Should we do it in order? It's cold today. A wet cold; not like winter in the Midwest, where I'm originally from.

—Oh yeah? I'm from Illinois myself. Boston snow is

almost cozy—it has to be because of the harbor, and the Charles River.

—So…why psychology? At Harvard no less. Do Harvard psychologists make more money, are they more likely to get tenure?

—Well…my mother was schizophrenic. It started manifesting when I was in junior high. I threw myself into schoolwork, spent all afternoon, every afternoon, in the library, to stay away from her.

—Thus, Harvard.

—Well, she ended up being institutionalized, and committed suicide. There was a suit, and a settlement, and thus Tufts for my undergrad. I fell in love with Boston, so I decided to stay. There's even a joke: "Anyone can get into Harvard for *graduate* school!"

—Heh.

—How's the hand?

—It's…hurting.

—What's your book about?

—The Halloween parade in Salem, and the witch trials. The costumes take over the parade goers wearing them thanks to the curse of Tituba, and then…

—For Halloween last year I dressed like a sexy watermelon.

—A sexy *what*? That's hilarious.

—Yeah, it was a silly costume. A tube dress, a little slinky, very short, pink with a seed pattern and green trim on the bottom. And it had a bite taken out of the side. I had gotten rib tattoos—stylized wings—and wanted to show at least one of them off.

—I wonder how many Harvard grad students dress like

sexy, winged, watermelons?

—I'd guess…one. Just me. Your hand.

—Yes?

—It's red, almost purple.

—It hurts a lot. But it's not unbearable. Very little is unbearable, I've found. Human beings can bear a lot of pain. A lot.

—Well, the experience of pain is subjective. Even the expectation that pain will decrease can lead to pain decreasing.

—I always anticipate pain. Nothing but pain. A breeze passing over my skin is pain. The sun in my eyes is pain. My mind in the dark is nothing but pain.

—Is that…from your book?

—Sure it is.

—Okay.

—I bet you're not going to go to the library now to pick up a copy, eh?

—I have a lot of reading to do for my dissertation.

—No problem, I'm sure you do.

—I'm going to show you a Pain Rating Scale. Uh, there are little cartoon faces on this, but you can ignore them if you like. They're mostly for kids. Point to the face and number that most exactly describes the pain you are experiencing.

8

HURTS

WHOLE LOT

—You can pull up the bar and remove your hand at any time.

—I like the cartoon faces. Do people generally not cry until the pain hits 10?

—No, no. That's just for children.

—You do this experiment on *kids*?

—No. But the chart is for kids as well as adults. The faces are not supposed to represent a person's expression, but what they feel on the inside.

—Oh. In that case…

0

NO HURT

—Really?

—Yes. Now, you point to how much it hurt when you got your wing tattoos.

—Okay.

4

HURTS

LITTLE MORE

—But you sat there for hours. Hell, you paid for it. I'm at least getting twenty dollars for this, maybe more.

—I'm sorry, I thought I made it clear that you'll be getting twenty dollars no matter how long you can tolerate the pain. Would you like to stop now?

—Why did you get wing tattoos?

—Am I a distraction? Maybe you should concentrate on your hand.

—I can stay here for hours. Zero, no hurt! Remember?

Didn't the form I filled out promise that there'd be no permanent damage? You said the rod won't break the skin.

—It won't.

—Good. So we can look at one another in silence, or we can do something tedious, like talk about men, or you can tell me more about your tattoos.

—I got them with the settlement money.

—How much did it hurt when you got the settlement money?

—The proposed topic of discussion is your history of pain and pain management, not mine, sorry.

—Fine, I'll tell you about pain. This little rod you have digging into the back of my hand isn't anything. Remember the Marathon bombing?

—Were you there? Oh, your novel! Is that what your novel is about, really? Supernatural horror at some other public gathering, as a symbol for the real horror of that day.

—Are you a Harvard psychologist or a community college English major? Whether I was there doesn't matter. Did you see the picture? You must know the one I mean? He didn't feel a thing either, I'm sure. His nerves were blown away along with the flesh and bone of his leg. Then there was the tourniquet. It didn't hurt till afterward. Not only didn't that guy's leg hurt, nothing else hurt either. Whatever problems he had vanished in that moment. Athlete's foot, a sore shoulder, overdue bills.

—He's likely in plenty of pain now.

—Ain't we all?

—Are you? Point to the face and number that most exactly describes the pain you are experiencing.

NO HURT

—Okay, still zero. Good to know. What's the most pain you've ever experienced?

—I was in the hospital one time. When I lived in Chicago. I had some problems back then. Want to hear about them?

—How funny. We can talk about whatever you like about, within reason, during the experiment.

—Oh, never mind then.

—Huh?

—You said "within reason." What I have to tell you isn't reasonable.

. . .

—I was in the hospital because I was in pain. It was a blood-pain.

—"Blood pain"?

—That's what I called it anyway. I even used the term in my novel. It's pretty creepy, right?

—Right. Sure.

—Blood pain is the pain created by black blood cells pulsing through your veins and arteries. That's how I always imagined the blood-pain anyway. Something rough and sharp, like glass dust in your veins.

—But black?

—Like tiny shards of obsidian or something, slicing and slicing.

—Did you see a hematologist or a…

—Psychologist, yes. Who referred me to a psychiatrist. But only after I took a cheese grater to my arm.

—Oh.

—My *other* arm, of course. You can roll up the sleeve and take a look, if you like. I'd show you myself, but I don't want to lose the experiment.

—I told you, you can't lose this experiment I'm sorry, Ms, uh, but we should end this. Of course, you'll get your payout.

—I don't want to end this yet.

—I'm going to.

—Your mother talked about you a lot, in the hospital. I was there for a few months.

—This is ludicrous.

—Your name is Joanne.

—That's on the briefing sheet.

—You love Shakira. Loved her anyway. My info is out of date. After all, it's been years.

—That's on Facebook. Those damn privacy settings are always changing. You could have Googled my name while reviewing the briefing sheet.

—She told you she hated you once when you were a girl. She used to hold your mouth open and spit down your throat to teach your stomach a lesson. She said that her spit was her soul and that this way she'd always be inside you.

—Okay.

—I didn't set out to find you or anything.

—Oh, is it all just a coincidence now? I should call security.

—No, I mean it. Everything I said is true. I need the money. Freelancing is a horrible way to live, especially in an expensive place like Cambridge. I have to pay for my own home heating oil too. It's like paying a thirteenth month's rent. I saw your photo a few weeks ago on the bulletin board, along with the other psych grad students. You look like her, you have her last name, you're the right age. I was here for another study. I decided I'd sign up to every experiment I could until I found you. I have something to tell you about her.

—Well, what do you have to say? Did my mother have some last words?

—"They're coming for me. The orderlies are coming for me." That's what she said.

—She was a paranoid schizophrenic. For all I know, you're also a paranoid schizophrenic.

—What if I told you that I saw something?

—Okay, what did you see?

—I saw two men, orderlies, walking past the window in my little room. All the doors have windows, of course, so they can do instant checks and so patients can't ambush the workers by hiding in a corner or something when the door starts to open. It was unusual that they'd be passing by so purposefully. The doors are all locked, which I am sure is against the law and is absolutely a fire hazard, so I mushed the side of my face against the window so that I could see. They had a little tray, opened the door to her room, rolled it in, and locked the door again. They didn't even go in.

—Yes, I know all that.

—What?

—My mother slashed her belly open. Obviously she had to have some access to some tool or blade.

—Yes, but...

—Have you been in pain, all these years, thinking of what you'd seen?

—It took me a long time to climb out of my own black

hole. And that made it even worse. What I'd seen.

—Sure, that's why most psych wards have been shut down. All sorts of terrible things happen there. It took my father a long time to find a proper one for my mother.

—But it *wasn't* a proper one, don't you understand?

. . .

—Don't you understand what I'm trying to say? Those staff members didn't leave your mother alone with a sharp because they were incompetent or stupid. I think they *wanted* her to kill herself. They went out of their way to make it possible. What? Don't you understand?

. . .

—Oh, come on. Don't push that stupid Pain Rating Scale at me again.

—Point to the face and number that most exactly describes the pain you are experiencing. You need your twenty dollars, don't you?

6

HURTS

EVEN MORE

—Good. Now let me tell you something. I had to do a lot of favors, I had to do a lot of *things* to get where I am today.

—What are you talking about?

—Isn't that how it goes in your dumb little novel? A practiced revelation, a public demonstration of so-called "evil." I bet it is. Genre fiction is full of clichés and cheap irony.

—Hey!

—Here's some psychology for you: you can never mask

the self. Pick a mask, you're just revealing yourself. You come in here and act all tough and weird, but that's just you trying to deal with your trauma by spreading it around. And I, on the other hand, put on a nice little face. Objective and concerned with social science. But my experience with psychology is far more personal. Up close and personal. I bet that in your novel you had the bitchy woman dressed like a witch, maybe some fat guy dressed like a gluttonous monster with a giant mouth. Did the town slut dress like a sexy watermelon, or Elvira? The local bullies were skeletons and Frankensteins. And I'll also bet the nice girl ended up playing Good Fairy Princess and saving some little kids in superhero costumes or something.

—So your wing tattoos…

—I never felt freer than I did after I got my way.

—Oh, I get it now.

—…you do?

—Orderlies don't get paid very much, and frankly, most of them look like they've been hit in the face with a shovel every morning before work. A nice white girl ready to do anything for them, and in exchange all they had to do is make a tool available to your mother. That was the plan, and look, it worked. You're almost successful, and almost normal. Almost.

—No. I mean, it's not my fault. Not completely. She could have decided not to commit suicide, after all. She could have slept through the night and the morning check-in would have found the blade and she would have been fine. *Fine*. But she wanted to. She wanted to. Suicide is just another form of pain management.

—You know, there are many forms of pain management.

I learned that the hard way, inside. Writing helps me. Drinking helps writers. Taking a drive with the windows open helps drinkers.

—I can call security. Wouldn't it be like something out of a bad novel if the security guards looked just like the orderlies in your old psych ward? But I'm not going to. I'm going to just lift the rod off your hand, like so, and ask you to point on the Pain Rating Scale to how you're feeling right now.

—You can call security if you like. You think I'll be less free back in the boobie hatch? You think you'll be any freer with a fancy PhD and a tenure track job at some little liberal arts college in Ohio? Tell me again about masks and the self, why don't you?

—Look, just let me get one last datum, and I won't call security, and you'll get your twenty dollars, and then you can go home and call the cops and explain that you, a poor horror writer with a psychiatric record and no proof, want to have me, a Harvard grad student with a nice bank account and lots of social capital and, frankly, a great pair of tits I inherited from my mother, arrested for secretly having my suicidal schizophrenic mom killed.

—It's funny that you think I'd call the cops. That I'd even have to call the cops. My work here is done.

—Oh look, you pointed to the face with the tears running down its cheeks. It looks just like you. *Hurts Worst.* A perfect ten.

—We're holding hands, you know.

—So we are.

THE DOOM THAT CAME FROM PORTLAND
Nathan Carson

Recommended Pairing: **Cascade Bourbonic Plague**

It was on Independence Day 2014 that I got the call. Our lead vocalist Uta Plotkin was on the line, a week away from her 33rd birthday, and she was letting us down easy. We had recently returned from our second European tour, a trip which took us from Norway to Greece and set us on a stage at Hellfest in rural France on a bill that was topped by Iron Maiden, Aerosmith, and Black Sabbath—the biggest show any of us had ever played. We were slated to tour North America next at the end of August as main support to Nik Turner's Hawkwind. It would be our last trip with Uta.

I'd be lying to pretend there was no tremor of panic or disillusionment in our ranks. Our bass player, who I will refer to here as Dingus (a nickname he coined himself), immediately gave his notice as well. But my partner Rob Wrong had co-founded Witch Mountain with me way back in July of '97. At that time doom metal was perhaps the least cool musical style any Portland band could consider performing. We'd been through some very low lows over the last seventeen years but also had a very long range plan. The first step was simply to get through this next tour, having as much fun and enduring as little psychological scarring as possible.

Putting our best foot forward, we four Mountaineers rented a minivan. I renegotiated the deal online 48 hours before the trip and saved us $600. We subsequently hit the road with minimal equipment, maximum merchandise, a big bag of weed, and smiles on our faces. Since the drive to Oakland is long and taxing, we had reserved a campsite outside Ashland, OR. That split the trip nicely, and gave us a chance to spend our first night stargazing, eating out of the cooler we'd filled on my food stamp dime in Eugene, and smoking the green at a furious pace—we have a longstanding rule that we do not enter Arizona, Texas, or Utah with any controlled substances. The first gig went smoothly. The bands were musically quite different, but as hoped, seemed to compliment each other nicely. Nik Turner's Hawkwind was "far out" enough for the Witch Mountain fans, and we were tuneful enough to not scare away the graying duffers that came out in droves for a fix of *Space Ritual* and "one of everything" at the merch table.

After the gig, as we were headed to sleep on a friend of a friend's floor. I had demanded a quick run to the Mission

District for an after-show burrito. This is more than tradition. I consider it mandatory. The pilgrimage to El Farolito makes me salivate, even as I type this--a shameful reminder that Portland is far closer to Canada than Mexico. After gorging on a chicken and shrimp wrap the size of my lower leg, I guided our gleaming minivan onto a sidewalk parking space in front of the house where we were to smoke, drink, and ultimately, sleep.

Show number two took place at the infamous Viper Room in Hell-A. I have grown very fond of Los Angeles over the years, but it is still one strange beast of a scene that is continually unpredictable and only occasionally rewarding. Of particular note this night was nothing that happened on the tiny corner stage we all somehow managed to squeeze onto, but rather the VIPs in attendance. First I was introduced to Carmine Appice—the infamous drummer from Vanilla Fudge and countless other classic rock groups. Then Jello Biafra showed up. He and I have always gotten along well, so it was great to see him kicking it with Nik Turner, and joining the band on stage. I'm told that Lisa Marie Presley was also there, but alas, I never crossed paths with her.

Tucson was particularly memorable for me because the older brother of my childhood best friend was in attendance. I'd first met Jayson Rockey when I was four years old. He was the kid who lived in the next town over (Albany, OR, then later, Salem) who sported a mullet, drove a muscle car, and turned me on to both D&D (age 10) and LSD (age 14).

Perhaps more pertinently, Jayson also gave me a cassette of Ozzy Osbourne's *Speak of the Devil*—a double live album comprised entirely of Black Sabbath songs that was one of my first gateways along the path of doom. It was a treat to see my old friend, and to shout out to him from the stage—a stage I might never have set foot on had he not helped lead me into the darkness at such a young age.

Next night in Albuquerque, we returned to the Launch Pad, a venue Witch Mountain had not played since 2003. After the gig, the promoter offered to host both bands, which was a swell thing to do and the first opportunity that NTH and WM had to really get to know each other. The promoter was experiencing some domestic infelicity with his wife due to her not wanting him to drive home intoxicated. We made a plan to follow her back to the homestead, but she left in such a huff and drove so fast that she actually lost us.

So we meandered back to club and instead followed our besotted host as he wove home in his pick-up truck. When we finally arrived, he admitted that one particularly dramatic swerve we'd witnessed from a safe distance was the exact moment that he'd puked on himself while driving. Ultimately, we ended up camping-in with the other band, filing into the house like sweaty sardines. The promoter's wife had cooled down enough to prepare us some hot food, and much smoking and drinking and carousing commenced.

There ain't shit between Albuquerque and the oasis of Austin, TX, so we took a day off to make the long drive. Austin is always a treat and Red 7 is a killer venue. Earlier in the evening, Witch Mountain had been treated to a four star meal, compliments of our friend Matt Walker of the band Unmothered. His day job as floor manager of an upscale Italian restaurant paid dividends and we enjoyed bottles of wine, and platters of steak, fish, and ghoulishly gluttonous desserts. Sadly, all of our leftovers remained in the backstage fridge at Red 7 as we loaded out in a flurry of chaos and flaring tempers. We were officially one week in.

New Orleans was our next stop and it was the longest drive of the tour that hadn't been budgeted for with a day off. So Rob and I suggested we just make the trip overnight and arrive early. Uta took first drive and eventually pulled us into a Denny's parking lot around 5am. I had pledged to take over if I could grab a milkshake and a Superbird sandwich. But somehow the communication had broken down already. Dingus was flipping out that his back hurt and he couldn't spend another minute in the van. Uta seemed to have forgotten that we made a plan to get to NOLA early. The quitting half of the band demanded a hotel room and NOW. So I sat alone enjoying a mediocre Denny's meal by myself then booked us a room next door where we could sleep for a few hours before the cleaning lady kicked us out.

Thankfully, New Orleans turned out to be quite the balm for our fraying spirits. In the nick of time we chanced upon one of the best and largest crowds of the entire tour. I would never have expected it on a Tuesday night in NOLA, but the show room at the ironically named Siberia club was absolutely packed from wall to wall. The crowd—quite used to staying up til dawn on Bourbon Street and beyond--didn't want Nik to quit. He serenaded the crowd with solo sax renditions of "Tequila" and "When the Saints Go Marching In" simply to appease them. Both bands sold a grip of merchandise and good times were had by all. Uta had spent all winter in that city, so she was carried off early by friends and her lover. In the morning we found her at her favorite coffee shop, sleepy, smiling and refreshed.

Birmingham, Alabama is home to one of the best small clubs in the country. The Bottletree was built by musicians, for musicians. It's got a great stage and sound, kitschy décor, and an Airstream trailer out back where bands like Witch Mountain tend to stay after the show. Unfortunately, it's nearly impossible to get a crowd out to see interesting music in Alabama and this was the lowest paying gig of the tour by quite a bit. Still, there was nowhere else to be that night. The Bottletree put warm Southern food in our bellies and a roof over our heads. It also provided the impetus for further astonishing conflict between bands.

Backstage, someone had left a pair of sunglasses that were coveted by Nik Turner's son Elfin (yes, that's his real name), who was a fit college lad on the road with his dad for the sake of "life experience." I was against him coming all along, but he turned out to be a decent guy and definitely did his part as roadie. As the NTH crew left the building that night, Elfin asked me to bring the sunglasses to him in Memphis if they were not claimed by their rightful owner. Instead, after he left, they were claimed by the Dingus, who cared not a whit about who might have coveted or lost them.

The morning after Memphis, we arose at the filthiest, most dog-hair infested house of the trip, and staggered toward Lafayette, GA—a farmland property host to the inaugural Meltasia music fest. It was a gorgeous, Southern summer night, with several huge outdoor stages set on rolling hills. There weren't a whole lot of people there, and the sound man kept referring to Uta as "Ms. Layne Stayley," but we did our jobs, and played our set, despite the air of heaviness brought by the news that our guitar player Rob Wrong's father had passed that afternoon at a hospital in Alaska. Rob was a trooper and played through his tears. As soon as we left the stage, we started driving to a hotel four hours closer to our next destination since we wanted to be early to sound check at our big festival gig in Raleigh.

Witch Mountain arrived promptly at the Hopscotch festival in Raleigh. This show was the anchor around which the entire trip had been booked. Hopscotch is an eclectic music fest in a nice North Carolinian college town, and extremely well organized. We were main support on a bill that included our old friends High on Fire as headliners. Immediately before us was SubRosa—a band we know and love, who had last supported us at the Hellfest in France.

That night was magical for WM. Major label metal success story Mastodon was also playing Hopscotch, and they dropped in to party with us backstage after our respective shows. Also, John Campbell—bass player of Lamb of God—drove down from Richmond to meet us. We all got along with him famously. It was a well run show, a huge crowd that loved our music, and I even had family in the house—my Aunt Vicky and her two daughters, my favorite teenage cousins Scarlet and Alexandria. One year those girls were awkward, home-schooled deer in headlights. The next, they were into anime cosplay, and moderating online forums for soft black metal acts like Cradle of Filth and Nightwish. I love those girls.

Baltimore and Philly were on a Monday and Tuesday, and they felt like it. Even on weeknights the combined draw of both bands kept any of the shows from being truly soul-crushing. But the tide turned crimson in Sellersville, PA. This affluent small town 45 minutes north of Philadelphia was host to a gorgeous small theater run by a professional volunteer staff—mostly retired folks who love progressive rock. It was an elegant place to present music such as ours, and we all appreciated the treatment. However…

However. It was here that Elfin made his move and stole back the sunglasses that Dingus had claimed for himself. Both were being childish. Neither of them had grown up poor. Either of them could have bought a nicer pair of sunglasses in a heartbeat. So on principle alone, they verbally sparred and seethed. I caught wind of the argument, and attempted to reason with both. Not only was my logic rebuffed, but Dingus decided that because I hadn't resoundingly sided with him that I deserved to "eat a dick" or "fuck off" as the case may be. I'm not used to any bandmate speaking to me this way and took it personally. But I took it. We still had a long way to go. In retrospect I do wish I'd taken the glasses and broken them in half.

After the show, not speaking a word to each other, Dingus drove us in to New York City, where we proceeded to pay $50 for a parking space so that he could stay the night in his mother's hotel room. We were graciously invited to sleep on the hardwood floor. Luckily, this is not my first rodeo, and I always carry an inflatable mat, sleeping bag, and separate pillows to go beneath my head and my knees. Along with ear plugs and a sleep mask I am good to go in nearly any situation. The next morning Rob Wrong and I took our brunch separate from the kids and dined and dashed from an upscale food court in lower Manhattan while Dingus' mother took the others shopping or whatever.

In our first ever New York show that wasn't in Brooklyn we played the basement room of Webster Hall. It was a fine gig and we were visited by producer Martin Bisi (Sonic Youth, Swans, Herbie Hancock), who stopped in just to see us. Our friend and photographer Marne Lucas also came out, as well as my friend Meeo, who Rob and I ended up staying with in an effort to spend as little time with Uta and Dingus as possible.

I try not to fault those two for the anguish they caused me on this tour. Whenever a relationship is coming to an end, people do and say things they don't really mean. When you give notice from a job, the last two weeks are hard. I'm certain that I did and said things that made their lives difficult as well. So when I open up about how much parts of this tour made me feel like Catherine Deneuve in *Repulsion*, please understand that these horrors did not inflict permanent damage.

Boston was a balm for me as it was there that I met up with Ms. Erin J.L. The Middle East club is a favorite of mine from several tour stops I've made over the years, but it was her childhood stomping ground. She brought out old friends, and we danced during Nik Turner's set and eventually escaped. I made a point to get the bands paid and loaded my own equipment out to the van before disappearing to Erin's hotel for a romantic rendezvous.

My band reconvened with me the following afternoon. Months later I was sent the parking ticket they incurred in my name while the rental van was in their charge. I suppose $35 is a small price to pay for a bit of peace and quiet and good loving. In Harvard Square, an aspiring young dancer in athletic gear practiced his original moves that blended modern dance and martial arts while I said, "Farewell-for-now" to Erin.

Back behind the wheel, I guided us out of mad Mass and into the woodlands of Vermont. There we took winding back roads through darkness and rain to enjoy our first night off in twelve days with my old friends Michael and Sarah. The couple were Reedie Portland ex-pats who found a house and paying work in rural Vermont and chose that place to have a child. It was great to have a home-cooked meal and see familiar faces. Likewise, the two (now three) had moved to such a remote locale that they were truly happy to have our company around their hearth.

Our border crossing into Quebec was smooth as usual, and the most noteworthy recollection I have of Montreal was that Nik Turner's rental van began having catastrophic issues. There was some sort of computer failure going on that meant the van could only be stopped and started six more times before going into some sort of failsafe mode. So they'd been forced to fill up on gas with the van running, cross the border with the van running, and make their stops count. It was highly stressful for all of us, and the rental company kept sending them on wild goose chases to waste time at repair shops that never did anything more than charge them money to lose sleep.

After the gig we stayed with a very friendly couple we'd met at our Ottawa show in 2012. They had a house with beds to spare for each of us and cooked us a bacon and egg breakfast in the morning. The kindness of the many people who took care of my band at various points along this tour cannot be underestimated.

Toronto was well-attended and our friend Sean from Blood Ceremony came out to support us. We had a good gig but I was distracted because the Lady Rebecca from Detroit had driven up to meet with me and booked a bed & breakfast for her and I that seemed plucked from the pages of a Harry Potter novel. The kitchen scene the next morning wherin a lame Brittanian of advanced age carved off morning sausage for us would have driven Terry Giliam into ecstasies.

For the next three days and nights, I was on my own recognizance with Rebecca, and out of the van with the others. They'd gratefully be enjoying more room without me and showed their thanks by rolling a special joint for my separate return trip to the US border.

There never really was a good moment to smoke that J and I mostly put it out of my mind. It was stuffed in a pocket of my duffel bag in the back of Rebecca's rental car and I just pretended to myself that if I forgot about it, it would go unnoticed. Of course, once we reached the border, the guard ordered us to pop the trunk just as a dog ran by. That hound flipped the fuck out and I began quietly apologizing to Rebecca for my mistake and promised to take the blame. The border guard took her keys and rummaged through my belongings while the dog howled. Incredibly, they found nothing, handed the keys back and sent us on our way.

It was a stupid mistake that I will never make again, but the best way to celebrate our freedom was to pull over and smoke the joint. I pointed toward an exit, guided us to the backside of a motel, promising Rebecca that there would be a good place to smoke somewhere. Around the rear of the building was a small white gazebo designated for "Smokers." There was no one around so we took it as a literal sign and sat there calming down from the adrenalin incurred during our brush with international incarceration. Puff, puff, pass. I left the roach in a conspicuous place for the next smoker to enjoy.

Back on the road, we regrouped with the bands at the Bug Jar in Rochester, NY. After our set, I was standing out front of the building cooling off when some sort of PCP-addled tweaker ran screaming straight for the club's facade. He head-butted the window at top speed, cracking it with the force of a bowling ball, then careened up the street, eventually collapsing in a heap of seizing limbs. That's Rochester for you.

Once again, I collected the money for both bands, loaded my gear out to the van, and left with a lady on my arm. I booked us a room about an hour outside of town and took us to a diner recommended by a tollbooth attendant. There we were served mythically huge portions of Greek food at 3am. We were the only people there besides a couple of cops. It felt like the first level of *Resident Evil*. I looked for potential weapons or other special survival objects on my way out. Perhaps it was a premonition of danger.

Back at the hotel, I received a barrage of texts from my housemate in Portland. Apparently our temporary subletters had turned aggressive and the police had been called. This was not news I wanted to receive at 4am while 2,700 miles from home. I was already in the process of breaking up with my girlfriend of three years. Two of my bandmates had put in their notice. My dad's leg had recently been amputated at the thigh. The last thing I wanted was to get into a text shootout with two crazy people whose only responsibility was to hold the fort in my absence.

Four years earlier, the Beachland Ballroom in Cleveland had been the site of my first date with Rebecca. I'd met her the night prior at an Agalloch show I was managing in London, Ontario, and invited her to be my guest the next evening. So it was bittersweet to end our rendezvous there, but also a bit poetic.

My Uncle Michael, cousin Jessica and her husband (the latter two being totally authentic Ozzfesters) showed up to this gig, a show which started late due to more mechanical snafus from the Nik Turner van. We were all running on fumes and the frayed ends of sanity. And there was still nearly two weeks to go. Who in their right mind would book 31 shows in 34 days? Oh yeah. The booking agent. Me.

I won't bore you with much more day-to-day minutiae from here. Partially because I was in such a state of depression by this point in the tour, that I don't remember a lot of vivid details beyond the scenery that passed by our windows. Chicago brought the visit of one of my best friends, Dave G, and then we said goodbye and were on to the metropolis of Rock Island, Illinois. On Milwaukee, on Saint Paul, on Donner and Blitzen. My relationship, band, and household were all simultaneously splintering at once.

It was a life I had chosen and I had no regrets or complaints.

The best part of being in a band is that time onstage, when time slows down and you are gifted with the powers of a super-being or demigod. But it's not simply a power trip. That is just a small part of the rapture involved with making music with your closest friends through the loudest and highest fidelity sound systems possible. It's like piloting Voltron. Every note and movement is given the scale of a skyscraper in an earthquake. It is pure joy and all the stress and sweat that goes into the other twenty-three hours of my day is worth it for this opportunity to inhabit another dimension of reality prized open by sheer creative force.

At no point did I give up on the band or our future. Our fourth and best album, *Mobile of Angels,* was set for release a few days after we got home. It would go on to garner the most critical acclaim we've yet received. By December, it was difficult to count the number of best-of-the-year lists that had included us. In the esteem of many publications, we'd made one of the best metal albums of the year.

Every single article and review bemoaned the departure of Uta Plotkin. So did Rob and I. As we sat at home, fragmented after half the band had left, we watched our album go to work for us. Rob and I had founded Witch Mountain seventeen years prior and gone from a footnote on the local scene to minor international glory. It was vindicating and of course Uta was the center of attention for almost all of our most recent success. It can only help springboard her to the next phase of her career, which I personally look forward to seeing. One of the worst things about being in this band is that I don't get many chances to watch Rob Wrong play guitar anymore. I wanted to play in a band with him because I immediately loved his playing from the first time I saw him with his old group, Iommi Stubbs, at EJ's in Northeast Portland back in 1996. At least now I'll likely have the chance to go hear Uta sing.

Throughout October, we reintegrated into our normal lives after a year of furious rehearsing, album recording, art preparing, merch designing, and extensive tours of Europe and North America. There was nothing on the horizon. No plans. Just a time to reflect and eventually reanimate. I was personally comfortable with taking a year off. I felt like racing to rebuild a new lineup would be tacky and counterproductive. Then the audition tapes started coming in.

People, almost all of them women, wanted this job. Witch Mountain was a household name, touring hard, releasing emotional and honest classic doom metal albums, and being talked about in Spin and on NPR. Word of mouth in the era of social networking makes lightning look slow. Within a matter of weeks we had a number of audition tapes. Most were very impressive. Before Uta had joined the band, we'd likely have been happy to work with any of these vocalists. But the bar was set very high and the spotlight had snared us. The stakes were such that we couldn't afford to make any moves that were simply adequate. And then we got an email from Kayla Dixon.

Kayla is young and unknown and staggeringly talented. By the time you read this, we'll have completed our first tour with her, in support of our old friends YOB—a long-running doom metal band from Eugene, OR, just awarded #1 Metal Album of 2014 by Rolling Stone.

I'd never have imagined that we'd be up and running this quickly but I can't complain either. Rob and I have been down in the trenches of the rock and roll scene for twenty-five years now. We have worked against the grain and persevered when it seemed there was nothing to hope for. But our music was the only thing that mattered. Now it seems to matter to a lot more people. And that is very beautiful. I feel fortunate that there are energies conspiring to keep us rocking. Because we will rock. And we will be better than ever before.

See you on the road.

LAIRD BARRON
Interviewed by Justin Steele

JS: You recently edited the inaugural volume of The Year's Best Weird Fiction. The definition of weird fiction seems to fluctuate depending on who is discussing it. What elements make a good weird tale? What is the difference between weird fiction and horror? If someone asked you what weird fiction was and you could only answer by handing them one book to read, which book would you choose?

LB: It's a broad category and one that exists, similar to horror, along a spectrum. Ghost stories and a vast cross section of fairytales are manifestations of the weird and comprise its nucleus. Strangeness and deviation from the norm are common denominators. Inexplicability, confusion. Horror and the weird overlap. Horror is concerned with dread, fear, and disgust. Harm is implicit.

The weird is a continuum that includes the buttoned-down psychodrama of Robert Aickman and Thomas Ligotti, the pulpy weird fantasy of Burroughs' John Carter series, Howard's Conan adventures, Shirley Jackson's paranoid fantasies, and panoplies of the baroque by Livia Llewellyn, Jeff VanderMeer, and Michael Cisco.

I'll cheat, because I can. The Brothers Grimm collected fairytales and The Dying Earth by Jack Vance. Lots of horror and violence in those selections and the weird doesn't always skew that way, but that's how I like it.

The concept of cosmic horror didn't start with Lovecraft, although many consider him to be a father figure of the genre. What makes cosmic horror so compelling that it has been revisited time and time again? Are there any trends in the sub-genre that you have noticed? What attracted you to using cosmic horror in your fiction?

The *Old Testament* is basically the *Necronomicon*. So long as we primates gibber at mysteries and subordinate ourselves to superstition we're going to wrestle with a fertile and largely unexamined obsession with cosmic horror.

A number of writers do cosmic horror one-offs to snag anthology sales, but I wouldn't say there are many who strongly specialize. The main trend I see is Lovecraft anthologies 24/7. Some of them are terrific, some are weaker, very little produces anything new. But there's a ton of it to sort through. The best work is being done by those who are interested in cosmic horror and less so with H.P. himself. Livia Llewellyn and Gemma Files bring a brutal eroticism to the genre. John Langan is deft with the metafictional aspect. Cody Goodfellow hits hard with a punk aesthetic.

Weird Fiction has always been a very rich field, yet only occasionally does it overtly break into the mainstream. Why do you think that is, and do you think this will change or is in the process of changing?

These things are cyclical. Entertainment has diversified. More readers, more viewers, more consumers, spread thin. Small presses and independent filmmakers are plugging in to the gaps left by the bigger fish. Some of the bigger fish are taking chances based on the successes of the small fry. This too shall pass.

Building on the last question, what are your thoughts on weird fiction and film? The majority of horror films seem to rely on worn tropes, while truly weird horror movies seem few and far between. What do you think are the prime examples of weird horror film, and why do you think there are not more of them?

Halloween; Carpenter's *The Thing; Gozu; Sauna; Cure; Beyond the Black Rainbow; Valhalla Rising; Kill List; Europa Report...*

The weird market seems relatively healthy. It's important to remember that we're talking about a niche. If the audience clamors for this type of material, we'll see more. As I said previously, these trends are cyclical. Horror and dark, dark drama are hot. Two or three years down the road is a mystery.

As of the time of this writing, you have three published short fiction collections, and two novels, with plenty more in the works. I've always found it fascinating when authors look at their bibliography and discuss some of their favorite stories, and how often that doesn't seem to line up with the fan favorites. Of all you've written, what are your personal favorites? Do any stories have more personal meaning compared to others?

"Parallax" is the best story I've managed to write from a technical perspective. That's an infinity loop of tightly woven strands. I worked on it for nine months. It was inspired by the Scott Peterson trial. I considered how the prosecution presented what sounded to my layman's brain an airtight case. Then the defense presented a series of accounts, incidents and red herrings that were compelling on the surface. A Schrodinger's Cat type of scenario where prosecution and defense are presenting the jury with alternate universes. In one the husband is a murder. In the other, he's an innocent victim of circumstance.

"—30—" is another I'm fond of. Its provenance is quirky—I wrote it as a raffle prize for the Shirley Jackson Awards and added it as an original to *Occultation*. Charles Manson and *Helter Skelter* were the stuff of boogeyman nightmares when

I was an adolescent. "—30—" taps into that and to some unpleasant experiences my family had while camping in the mountains in Alaska. Philip Gelatt, the man who wrote *Europa Report* is adapting it for a feature film; that marks the story as a milestone in my writing life.

I'm partial to some of the characters I've created in recent years--Jessica Mace, Johnny Cope, Miller. So, LD50, *Hand of Glory*, and *The Men from Porlock* are high on my list. I'm proud that the *Occultation* collection made OutWrite's list of best queer horror books, and am particularly satisfied that "Strappado" and *Mysterium Tremendum* are fan-favorites.

Several of your more recent stories veer from cosmic horror, utilizing more of a psychological horror approach. What prompted this change?

It was inevitable, although I think the change isn't particularly dramatic. My work usually foregrounds other elements. The crime or noir or adventure is front and center while the horror slinks in from the wings. I'm influenced by many writers who carved their way through a variety of genres. Cosmic horror is a more recent development—I was weaned on Golden and New Wave science fiction, pulp fantasy, historicals, and crime. John D. MacDonald, Robert Parker, Donald Westlake, Ian Fleming...a lot of those paperbacks were lying around the house and I enjoyed them.

Over the past twenty-five years or so, I've gravitated toward Martin Cruz Smith, Joseph Wambaugh, Gillian Flynn, and

James Ellroy. The psychedelic nature of Ellroy's prose and Smith's own artistry have influenced me.

Your next collection will be your Alaska-based fiction, a place where you grew up and spent many years. Why are you revisiting Alaska now, several years into your writing career?

Alaska, dogs, cold weather, and the wilderness, are at my core. My process is to interpret rather than devise. The return to Alaska through fiction has always been inevitable. It has taken me a long time to build the courage to crack myself open and perform a necropsy on the kid who lived and died in Alaska. Eastwood said he found it difficult to look at his younger self. I get it.

For me, just as it is for plenty of people, life is like an old times prize fight that lasted a hundred rounds. Life knocked me down a lot in my early days. Running the Iditarod on a shoestring isn't a cozy or particularly happy existence and ultimately I walked away. I moved to the Pacific Northwest and eventually got soft. Life punched me again four or five years ago. It took some real effort and real support from family and close friends to get up off the canvas. All I had left in the world was my old dog, older truck, and my work. So, I buckled down and started punching back.

Your work has received much acclaim over the years. What else, if anything, would you still like to achieve as a writer?

I'm grateful for the successes. I'm grateful for the support of numerous editors and publishers. I'm grateful to my readers for buying my books and spreading the word. It's a privilege to take part in a literary tradition. I'd like to glance over my shoulder someday and not see myself hanging in, keeping pace. I'd like to open the distance between what I can accomplish today and what I'll be capable of in a decade, two decades, however long I have left. If I'm able to keep moving, keep progressing, I'll get there.

You've blogged before about having a doppelgänger. What's the story behind your double, and what's your personal theory about it?

Yes, it's followed me around since my late teens in Alaska. On multiple occasions, people have sworn it was me they saw on the opposite side of town or in areas I'd never ventured. This happened a few times in Alaska and Seattle, less so over the past few years. Maybe he or it is lying low. Maybe he or it wants attention—I've written essays about my double and featured doppelgängers in recent work. Appeasement, perhaps.

I don't have a rational theory, although some irrational ones creep into my thoughts on occasion.

But, with apologies to Peter Straub: *Who do you think is telling this story?*

I'd like to thank you for taking the time for this interview. Are there any upcoming works you would like to inform readers about?

I've turned a new collection, *Swift to Chase*, over to my agent. Several stories are scheduled to appear in major anthologies, including S.T. Joshi's *The Madness of Cthulhu, Volume II*; Christopher Golden's *Seize the Night*, and projects by Paula Guran, Greg Kisbaugh, Lois Gresh, and Ross Lockhart.

CASCADE BREWING
Beer Reviews by Arlo Brooks

Kriek 2012

From the moment I popped my bottle of Cascade Kriek I knew I was in for a treat. A 2012 bottle, opened late December, 2014, I knew that by now the flavors had time to settle and figure out what exactly the heck they were doing. Done in a variation of the traditional Belgian Kriek, Cascade chose to age a mix of red ales in oak barrels and then added sour cherries and bing. The beer pours darker than I thought it would, a crimson red that fades almost black (?!) like a stout, but with the tiniest crimson shade when you turn the glass the right way. A fizzy ring of white slightly circles about 2/3 of the glass, leaving a barely visible line on just a fraction of the glass. The aroma is a deep, lactic, oaky sour, subtle and simple and without an overabundance of cherries. The flavor is of slightly shifting flavors of sour cherry, followed by an aggressive hint of vinegar that trails throughout the rest of the beer, followed by a lasting, complex hit of carbonation, green apple, oak, cherries, grape, citrus, and raspberry. The beer improves as it warms, largely ditching the vinegar burst in favor of a velvety, Belgian red texture that is smooth and rounds out the rest of the flavors neatly. The ending product is definitely delicious, luxurious and subtle.

The Vine 2012

The Vine is a strangely light brew, pouring like a lager or amber in color but generating almost no head, instead fizzling and bubbling all over the place for about ten seconds before mellowing out to no head whatsoever. The look of the beer lacks complexity; I could be looking at a flat Blue Moon. The aroma boasts a classic note of lactic sour, following up with heavy white wine overtones as well as faint notes of pear and apricot. I hate to say it, but the taste is disappointing. Cascade's style of mixing various blondes or tripels that have soured over time does not seem to create a full-bodied beer. Instead, this one's central character is watered down, evoking a mild wine with its inclusion of white grapes. A juicy carbonation hits first, then a nice backdrop of fruity, mild tartness and some vinegary funk. As the flavor fades an all-too-apparent Chardonnay note lingers on the tongue, only complementing the sourness by controlling it, cutting it off...

Sours already are more readily compared to wines than almost any other beer styles. The inclusion of white grapes in the brewing of this beer distracts and detracts, and the sourness is just not full enough for there to be a distinct beer character as opposed to the impression of a weak imitation of wine. Despite there being some to enjoy in The Vine (especially the juicy flavors and appropriate carbonation of the initial taste), I cannot come close to recommending it considering its price, although if given the opportunity to try it again as opposed to buying a bottle I certainly would not turn it down.

Bourbonic Plague 2012

Bourbonic Plague is a monster. Decadent, humongous, and original, this very dark ale contains shades of tan and ruby in the color, but showcases its darkness first and foremost as compared to other Cascade sours. Aromas are tart and yet also resemble a porter (kind of smells like a sour stout). Hints of cherry, bourbon, leather, maltiness, chewiness, red wine, port, oak, and a dash of spice hit the nose quick and wildly. If Cascade knows how to do something right, it's make a good smelling beer. The taste is a rich, wild, rollicking ride through various intense, polarizing flavors, all of which are decadent, hard-hitting, and complex. First there is a smooth, sweet cherry flavor, right from the get-go. This quickly moves into a full-on lacto sour, complete with Cascade's trademark lingering vinegar funk. Rounding out the sour flavors comes a quick downturn into surprisingly malty, dark territory; bourbon, brandy, booze, porter, vanilla, and oatmeal flavors show themselves in a very big way. The tartness returns, revealing that the central bourbon flavor is just a crazy turn on the same sour ride. Lots of lingering funk, cherry, bourbon and malt leave a lasting taste in the mouth. The flavors are almost too rich; the beer could use a little more drinkability. It's decadent and intense and comes out with two guns blazing. Perhaps could use a little subtlety. Nevertheless, a wonderfully rich brew to share.

Strawberry Ale 2012

I'd been seeing it in stores for so long, and it finally got me. Today I picked up a Cascade Strawberry, despite my disappointment with their Blueberry Ale. The cork popped off with resonance and force, almost like a bottle of champagne. Two seconds later and my hand is soaked in bubbles. By the time I've gotten the bottle to the sink the bubbling volcano has quickly fizzed out. The pour reveals a gorgeous orange blonde red color that couldn't be more aptly described than 'strawberry blonde.' Huge aromas of strawberries fill the room as I pour, and the ale lightly crashes and splashes with bubbles and fizz like a firework show before quickly mellowing out into just a thin white line. As the beer sits, you can still see bubbles running to the top even after a few minutes without movement. When I put my face to the glass, I can hear the beer bubbling; and boy, can I smell strawberries and yeast. In fact, that's about all I smell: very complex, champagney strawberry aromas that dance all over the place, with a backdrop of lactic bacteria and yeastiness.

I finally take a sip and WHOA! This is a superb sour ale. Lots of body and complexity to this one. The carbonation eases the beer through its separate phases and flavors with ease and yet the beer hits knows how to hit each note, in order, cleanly, and efficiently, almost like a musician. First, it's just strawberries, carbonation, and a little vanilla. Beautiful, complex ripe strawberry flavors match the pure and unique approach shown in the aroma. The first third of the taste almost is like a strawberry soda. Soon, though, are some corkscrews. A sour cherry-like hit stains the strawberry soda taste, and then there is a brief but refreshingly carbonated berry flavor followed by huge lactic/vinegary funkiness that melds perfectly with the bubbly nature of the brew, and leaves it with a long lasting and delicious fruity and refreshing tartness that is subtle and powerful, reminding me of green apples and blueberries. Overall, this is a fruit-flavored sour ale with a lot of character, subtlety, and care put into the sequence of flavors. Cascade's Strawberry Ale is a superb example of strawberries used liberally and wildly to make a beautiful and strange range of flavors.

Blueberry Ale 2013

Blueberry is the first Cascade I ever tried, and it was a big disappointment. I thought it was watered down, lacked body, and was generally weak. Gave it another try, and I find with lower expectations I enjoyed it quite a bit more. I still prefer every other Cascade I had (except The Vine, which I actually disliked) more, but it's the appearance and aroma that I enjoy Blueberry for the most. The bottle opens and detailed blueberry aromas come pouring out. I think this is the most intense blueberry smell I have gotten from a beer. It captures the complexities of the fruit, and pays tribute to its essence with an aroma that mixes with the lacto bacteria in a beautiful and complementary way. Also the color and pour are gorgeous! The beer is a light pink or a dark red as you look up the glass. Lots to enjoy in terms of the visual aspects. The flavor is good, but not great: it's got a bit too much of a champagne feeling. Lack of flavors to define the body are what cause the major downfall of this beer. It just isn't full-bodied enough. The ending blueberry note is satisfyingly pleasant and floral, with some rosey flavors and some oakiness. In general I feel the middle section of the beer needs work. The lack of body leaves the beer feeling a bit watery.

Figaro 2013

I kind of like that Cascade calls their sour ales 'Northwest style.' So many breweries that specialize in sour beer tend to want to emphasize sour beer's origin in Belgian countries; I like that Cascade boldly rejects this notion, claiming the Northwest to have its own style of sour. Figaro definitely recalls elements of other styles of sour such as the Gueuze and the Berliner Weisse, but it also has characteristics that are wholly its own.

When I popped the cork of my 2013 Figaro, there was once again that distinct feeling that makes you know you are opening a Cascade beer: a heavenly scent fills the entire room, and quickly. In this case, it was a beautiful floral note mixed with an aroma of figs, lemons, heavy oakiness, lacto sourness, and a hint of raisin. While I was so mesmerized by the sublime odor, I failed to notice the beer overflowing out of the top of the bottle on to my hands, which is another thing that marks a Cascade beer. (I'm kidding, but it has been a trend!)

The pour of the beer is beautiful and simple. Orange and yellow mix together to make a beautiful sunlit color. A small line of head resonates.

Which brings me to the taste, which is quite a taste to behold. With several other Cascade beers I have reviewed here, there were clear phases to the flavors; one taste would arrive, swell, and then depart as another approached to take attention. Figaro is a bit different, and I can taste all of the flavors quickly overlapping with each other in a whirlpool of mouth-puckering deliciousness. Cascade must have figured out a way to use Chardonnay flavors to their advantage by the time they were making Figaro in 2013 (The Vine 2012 notably used white wine flavors to diminishing effect). Chardonnay certainly accents the opening flavors of this beer, and brings awareness to the complexity about to unfold. There is a sharp, lemon-like tartness that dominates the beer and fades into that strange vinegar/funk/slight bitterness/whatever you want to call it that is becoming a trademark of Cascade sours to me. There is a background presence of figs, grapes, lemon, lime, and citrus.

It's just a really tasty, drinkable sour, with its base in the influences of white wine and lemon. Unlike The Vine, the sour body is complex and really makes the beer memorable. This beautiful and intricate sour was my favorite Cascade I've tried.

BOOK REVIEWS

The Natural Dissolution of Fleeting-Improvised-Men:
The Last Letter of H.P. Lovecraft by Gabriel Blackwell
Civil Coping Mechanisms
Reviewed by Justin Steele

Gabriel Blackwell's book is a heady blend of gonzo, metafiction, madness and Lovecraftiana with the creep factor dialed up to ten. Taking the form of Lovecraft's final missive, *The Natural Dissolution of Fleeting-Improvised-Men* has Blackwell fearlessly inserting himself as the editor, bleeding madness and paranoia onto every page.

The book opens with the introduction which explains Blackwell's circumstances and purpose. A search for a missing girlfriend sees Blackwell living in a shelter in an unfamiliar city, taking daily odd jobs to keep from being homeless, when he makes a bizarre discovery. While shredding hospital records he finds a file on an ancestor, a man with whom he shares his name. Inside the file is a long letter to his namesake from pulp horror author H.P. Lovecraft. What follows is an obsession which brings Blackwell to the brink and leaves him a broken man.

The bulk of the book is the letter itself, with extensive footnotes by Blackwell which tell his own story in more detail. This narrative choice makes for a dense read, as a single footnote will go on to cover several pages, and the letter itself doesn't have paragraph breaks, making everything run together, taking two insane, rambling narratives and entwining them to become a mind-shattering whole. As it continues, the narrator's tale mirrors Lovecraft's in several ways, getting to the point where it is difficult to tell the two apart.

Blackwell may have written the best Lovecraftian work to date. The paranoia and madness are infectious, leaving the reader disoriented and reeling, as if they just finished reading the diary of a madman. This is a book that will be long remembered.

I Called Him Necktie by Milena Michiko Flašar
New Vessel Press
Reviewed by Gabino Iglesias

Sometimes a concept can make a novel work despite it having an otherwise unremarkable plot. Such is the case of Milena Michiko Flašar's _I Called Him Necktie_. The book tells the story of a young man living as a hikikomori, a term used in Japan to name extremely reclusive, antisocial individuals. The author's knack for dialogue, bizarre-yet-multidimensional characters, and great pacing would make this a great story anyway, but the way the main character rediscovers life and the way Flašar framed her entire narrative on a young man dealing with a very real and arguably very modern phenomenon is what pushes this novel into must-read territory.

Taguchi Hiro has spent the last two years of his life living as a hikikomori, very rarely leaving the limited space of his room and doing everything in his power to evade his own family as well as all other human interaction. Then, conscious of the way his behavior is affecting both his sanity and everyone around him, he decides to ve—in his parents' home in Tokyo. Taguchi tentatively decides to reenter the world, but does so with the apprehension and carefulness of someone entering a really cold body of water. Instead of joining the busy streets of Tokyo, Taguchi spends his days looking at the world from the relative safety of a park bench. There's a man who's always at the park, and sharing that space eventually brings Taguchi and the man together. The man is Ohara Tetsu, a typical middle-aged salaryman who has been recently fired and hasn't been able to tell his wife about the situation. Instead, he gets dressed every day, grabs his lunch, and sits at the park for the eight hours he's supposed to be at the office. With entire days full of nothing to do and strange reasons for being there, Taguchi and Ohara slowly get to know each other and discover a bond that goes beyond their individual circumstances and that hopefully can help them start a new chapter in their lives.

Being a hikikomori is one of those bizarre psychosocial ailments that seem to thrive in societies where constant/frenzied human interaction is a sine qua non element of urban living. Taguchi's character is unique because he has his own reasons for becoming one and for breaking out of his situation, but he also represents a large group of youngsters for whom society and its common practices are just too much to handle. While becoming a recluse and ignoring your family might be things that are generally frowned upon, the way Flašar presents society and the self-conscious way in which Taguchi seems to constantly deconstruct himself in order to understand his feelings are two elements that come together to make him a very likeable character whose reactions to life in the city are perfectly understandable.

While Taguchi would easily be enough to make this an interesting read, Ohara adds a second layer of richness and social commentary that makes the novel a necessary read. Instead of directly criticizing Japanese customs, the author created a character that serves as a vehicle to show the flaws of a society where your occupation defines you as a person. For the salaryman, not being a man who goes to the office every morning is the equivalent of not being alive anymore. He is ashamed of his unemployment and invents an entire life just to retain his wife's respect, which he thinks is based on his ability to provide rather than on everything else that makes him an individual.

I Called Him Necktie is a fast-paced, interesting read that looks at the way the systems we have created affect those who have to live inside them but are ill equipped to do so. With very short fragments instead of chapters and the author's knack for conveying action and feeling through dialogue, this novella is a sharp exploration of what it means to be a part of two very different circles of Japanese society and, ultimately, a short study of what it means to find yourself in a loud, hyperconnected world.

Outdancing the Universe by Lauren Gilmore
University of Hell Press
Reviewed by Gabino Iglesias

Lauren Gilmore's *Outdancing the Universe* is an unapologetically personal poetry collection that manages to hook readers with its wit and honesty and then violently pulls them into a strange world full of memories, movement, and feelings from which there is no escape and no desire to find it. From travelling to the ever shifting meaning of home, Gilmore slashes her past open with words and pulls out the strangest, shiniest, sharpest, most painful bits and shares them in a series of poems that show what happens when straightforward storytelling and outstanding poetry simultaneously occupy the same space.

While writing about the self is something most authors do in one way or another, the truth is that young authors have a harder time pulling it off due to a plethora of reasons that range from lack of experience and coagulated beliefs to not enough writing experience and still being caught in the very important search for their voice. In Gilmore's case, whatever separates fresh voices from that well-lived feel of found in outstanding older authors seems to have vanished:

I don't know when
wanderlust started collecting in my shoes like rain
in hurricane gutter pipes. Or why the only

place I have ever felt homesick is with my elbows
on my own kitchen table, I have always slept best
between mile markers. Every step

a miniature departure, I walked forward
into line with the other passengers, becoming
the same kind of no one as everyone else.

For Gilmore, home is a feeling, a state of mind, and
not a place. This is stated in *Outdancing the Universe* time
and again, but never the same way. Likewise, physicality is
acknowledged, but the themes that serve as the cohesive
elements of the collection all exist in the intangible space
between the real now and what the mind remembers of
the past. The poet is caught between past and present and
memories are both the oppressive forces that propel her
forward and the anchors that allow her to find some measure
of comfort and stability in her identity. Interestingly, this
identity is presented as they are in real life; ever-changing
and constantly (re)interpreted instead of monolithic. And
when that (re)construction doesn't work, fiction and/or
love enter the equation:

I fell in love daily. Four times
before breakfast. It is the most beautiful
method of forgetting yourself.

Outdancing the Universe is a text born of an artist trying
to make sense of the places and spaces, both geographical
and emotional, that she has inhabited and that, in various

degrees, helped shape her. The only critique that can be made, if any, is that the text is too short (which is a critique caused mainly by the reader's desire to devour more of Gilmore's work) and feels blatantly open-ended. However, the second the bio rolls around and the reader is informed that the mature voice they have just enjoyed was born in 1996, both of those vanish and what is left is a sense of having just experienced a gifted voice that deserves to be called outstanding despite being in the first stages of what promises to be a superb poetic journey.

The Castaway Lounge by Jon Boilard
Dzanc Books
Reviewed by Art Edwards

There's something about 20th century literature I will always miss: the centeredness of it; the sense of centuries of foundation lying under every word; Hemingway's deep, patient voice. I say miss because in 2013 I made a point to re-read two personal favorites, *Herzog* by Saul Bellow and *One Hundred Years of Solitude* by Gabriel Garcia Marquez. The experience of re-reading these two masterworks I found a little boring. I didn't respond to the words, which had sold me on literature decades ago. It felt, sadly, like they belonged to the past. Somehow, mind-bogglingly, the news hadn't stayed news. In an attempt at preservation, I'm not going anywhere near the Rabbit Tetrology.

Despite its proximity in style to the 20th century masters, no such boredom creeps in during the reading of *The Castaway Lounge* by Jon Boilard. We are immediately wrapped up in character and intrigue—a recession-ridden New England town in 1986; two roustabouts, Applejack and Hoyt, setting fire to a lake in the middle of the night. Applejack, our central concern in the novel, battles his inner demons as he acts out in a world of strip clubs, alley fights, and any type of addiction you can name. Boilard writes of Applejack sleeping with an unnamed woman, an act that occupies the grey area in his relationship with stripper/prostitute Suzanne:

> She wants it rough so that's how he gives it to her. It's a sweaty and athletic and sometimes violent romp. Afterward they drink warm, rusty water directly from the faucet near the washer and dryer and they rest and the wind outside is an unholy ghost. The woman kneels beside the mattress and says a soft prayer and it unsettles him.

While Boilard's writing style may have more in common with the two great Els of 20th century American mystery, Elmore and Ellroy, there is also something literary about this work—the back and forth of the telling between past and present, the measured cadence of the prose. Not to mention the description, which subject- and style-wise is just across the plain from Cormac McCarthy. Boilard writes of a confrontation between Applejack's friend Nick and the bible-thumping painter Scotch:

> Nick is small but he has boxing chops. He's focused and efficient and appears to be treating this like a routine workout. Scotch spits blood

and vomits, splattering Nick in the process. In the end Scotch is barely conscious, and with his mouth all tore up it looks like he just won a blackberry pie-eating contest.

The calm delivery gives the sense there is no real winner here. There is only staying less bloodied than the guy next to you, which will be you soon enough.

If Applejack can make one thing right before going south, it's avenging the death of the young girl Peanut, whose body parts keep cropping up around the fringe of town. Boilard writes:

> Peanut's leg is in tatters because critters have been messing with it, Applejack figures. Coy dogs and big cats and such. Boy makes a face as Applejack fetches it, gets it up on the bank, and rests it gently on a dark carpet of leaves. Boy gets sick on his own two feet and then apologizes to Applejack.

Despite this gruesome world—and it only gets moreso as the plot unfolds—there is hope for Applejack and his ilk, but can he punch, drink, and fuck his way to redemption, or justice for Peanut? As Jenny Two Drinks says: "You can't change who you are unless you change what you do." For Applejack, that's the hardest fight of all.

If I find one thing missing from *The Castaway Lounge*, it's a less subtle personal connection between Boilard and his work. I found myself wanting to know his reasons for writing the story, what makes it so important for him to tell. The Flaubert narrator-as-clear-pane-of-glass approach has its merits—and maybe I'm addicted to the more direct connection between novel and author that's become *de rigueur* in 21st century work—but that dimension is nowhere to be found in this tale, leaving Boilard with a missed opportunity to engage his reader. In short, I wanted more than Applejack's skin in the game.

The fading of the old masters has me realizing that the only way to feel reborn through literature is to find new writers who update the form for our generation. Patrick deWitt, Wells Tower, and Zadie Smith all fit the bill. I, for one, will also look for the next Jon Boilard. So much of *The Castaway Lounge* falls right into place for me.

The Scarlet Gospels by Clive Barker
St. Martins Press
Reviewed by Marc E. Fitch

Clive Barker's return to horror fiction with the release of *The Scarlet Gospels* was one of the biggest events in horror fiction this year. Barker has remained one of the most influential figures in both horror fiction and film, with his *Books of Blood* collection setting the standard for what a short fiction collection could be. His bloody imagination appeared to know no limits as he ventured into territory outside the bounds of Stephen King and brought the mass market along with him. That is why I kept reading *The Scarlet Gospels* long after I would have closed the book on any other writer.

The Scarlet Gospels was billed as the death of Barker's

infamous Cenobite, Pinhead. To pay our respects we follow occult detective Harry D'Amour and his friends into Hell as he attempts to rescue his longtime friend and blind ghost-whisperer, Norma Paine. Pinhead is attempting in Hell what Lucifer attempted in Heaven—a coup—and, for reasons unknown, he wants Harry to witness his ascent to power. To coax the reluctant Harry, he kidnaps Norma, forcing Harry and three of his unique friends to follow him into the underworld. Pinhead carves a bloody path through Hades and Harry follows hot on his heels. The journey comes to resemble a funeral procession—but not for Pinhead.

It was difficult to come to terms with *The Scarlet Gospels*. Barker has been a great inspiration and is truly a giant of the genre. But his latest novel reads like the work of an adolescent coming to horror for the first time. The dialogue is especially grating and juvenile. One would think that a group of people wandering through the horrors of Hell might be, well, horrified. Instead they banter with sexual innuendos, bad jokes and one-liners straight out of an eighties action movie. Harry's predilection for magic allows him to move virtually unharmed through what is supposed to be the worst that God has to offer. It's too easy. It's too laid back. It doesn't retain the tension, suspense or dread that is supposed to be the mark of horror fiction. Even the scenes that are meant to be squeamish come across as uninspired, like the upteenth sequel of a horror movie that was once great.

But there are glimpses of the old master. His imagining of Hell is unique—a parallel universe complete with cities, classes of citizens and political tensions. Barker summons his talents for the final act in which Pinhead finally reaches

Lucifer's castle and takes the throne of Hell. For this—for his imagining of Lucifer's tragic, anguished and eternal life, the previous two hundred and fifty pages and the meandering end are worth it.

I can't say that the majority of this work didn't disappoint me but I also remain haunted by Barker's depiction of Lucifer and the ruin of Hell. Most haunting of all may be the mind that conceived it.

Selected Tweets by Tao Lin & Mira Gonzalez
Short Flight/Long Drive
Reviewed by Jay Slayton-Joslin

In 2012, Jonathan Franzen stated his theory of how Twitter, ebooks and the internet is bad for writing and the creation of art. In 2015, acclaimed writers Tao Lin & Mira Gonzalez showed Franzen where to put that theory with the publication of *Selected Tweets*.

Selected Tweets (published by Short Flight/Long Drive—a division of respected journal *Hobart*) is an accumulation of the best tweets published by both writers over years on their various Twitter pages. The book works best for those who are familiar with the authors' work. Lin's tweets find obsessions and humor (as well as despair) in the mundane boredom that most writers deny the existence of. Those who are familiar with his earlier works (*Taipei, Shoplifting From American Apparel*) will quickly realize that *Selected Tweets* is no different from the autobiographical novels he has written before. The layout may seem strange, or compared to some of Lin's books, normal, but it is impossible to say that the collection of tweets is stranger than Lin's debut novel, *Eeeee Eee Eeee*, which featured talking dolphins. Equally, fans of Mira Gonzalez's writing would quickly be familiar with the same combination of sex, drugs and apathy for the offline world that was featured in her collection *i will never be beautiful enough to make us beautiful together*. The authors compliment each other remarkably well. The book acts as a flipbook, one half dedicated to one author, the other revealing their most personal thoughts, sometimes correlating with each other, mentioning other authors and presses in a way that acts as a diary for the years they logged.

The only issue with *Selected Tweets* is that it is difficult to imagine it escaping out of the conditions that it was born in. The book will undoubtedly be successful due to the fan base that Gonzalez and Lin have cultivated in (and out) of the Alt Lit community. The book will be well received not just due to its writers, but because of the raw honesty that people in similar states of minds identify with, a state not found in popular fiction. Ultimately, *Selected Tweets* is not as strong as either of the authors' standalone work, but together Lin and Gonzalez capture enough of their interesting personalities to counteract each other's weaknesses. *Selected Tweets* is an interesting artifact, representative of the 21st century, one of the most innovative periods in literature and publishing, but the words that are on the page are not as interesting as the ideas they represent. Still, with the tweets chronicling a cast of literary names, books and insights into the personal lives of two great authors, *Selected Tweets* is like a good B-sides and rarities album—not quite amazing as a regular release, but damned better than the silence in between those works.

Arlo Brooks is a writer and musician from Pasadena, California.

Nathan Carson was raised by loving pagans on a goat farm in the rural backwoods of Oregon. A steady diet of D&D, LSD, and incredibly strange music made him the man he is today: a professional writer, DJ, and founding drummer of internationally acclaimed doom metal band Witch Mountain. His debut novel, *Starr Creek*, will be published by Lazy Fascist Press in 2016.

Allison Floyd lives in Boise (which is in Idaho, not Iowa). Her work has appeared in *The First Line, The Review Review, Bitch Magazine,* and *TOSKA Magazine,* among others. Her latest failed attempt to blog can be found at allisonmfloyd.com. She is currently seeking a publisher for her experimental short novel entitled *Bluebeard's Bel-Air Bachelor Pad*, which is a mash-up of Reality T.V., Rock and Roll tropes, and the classic fairy tale.

Daphne Gottlieb stitches together the ivory tower and the gutter just using her tongue. She is the award-winning author of ten books including the new collection of short stories, *Pretty Much Dead*. Previous works include *Dear Dawn: Aileen Wuornos in her Own Words,* a collection of letters from Death Row by the "first female serial killer" to her childhood best friend. She is also the author of five books of poetry, editor of two anthologies, and, with artist Diane DiMassa, the co-creator of the graphic novel *Jokes and the Unconscious*. Daphne is the winner of the Acker Award for Excellence in the Avant-Garde, the Audre Lorde Award for Poetry, the Firecracker Alternative Book Award, and is a five-time finalist for the Lambda Literary Award. She lives in San Francisco.

Nick Mamatas is the author of several novels, including *Love is the Law*, and the forthcoming *The Last Weekend* and *I Am Providence*. His short fiction has appeared in *Best American Mystery Stories*, *Asimov's Science Fiction*, *Trigger Warning. US*, and many other venues. Nick also works full-time as an editor. His most recently anthology, co-edited with Masumi Washington, is the international science fiction/crime hybrid *Hanzai Japan*.

Tiffany Scandal is the author of two books, *There's No Happy Ending* (Eraserhead Press) and *Jigsaw Youth* (Ladybox Books). Her fiction and nonfiction has been published in *Vol. 1 Brooklyn*, *Ladyblog*, *The Magazine of Bizarro Fiction*, *Living Dead Magazine*, and a handful of anthologies. She has also read for the RADAR Production Reading Series, a San Francisco based organization founded by Michelle Tea that features the best in emerging and underground writers. She currently resides in Portland, Oregon with three black cats.

Justin Steele is the co-editor of the anthology *The Children of Old Leech*, a Shirley Jackson Award finalist. He is also the fiction editor of *Strange Aeons* and founder of *The Arkham Digest*. He lives in Delaware.

Tania Terblanche is a writer from Pretoria, South Africa, where she works in engineering to fuel her ideas for worlds and artefacts that don't exist yet and to season her in creating systems of her own. She is currently completing her MA in Creative Writing at Rhodes University and loves stories because they are secret and beautiful and sometimes more true than anything.

Thank you for reading *Lazy Fascist Review*. We hope you enjoyed this issue and look forward to catching up with you again. Until then, please track down more work by the incredible authors featured in this issue. If you have any comments or want to talk about beer, fishing, *Lazy Fascist Review*, or anything else that's on your mind, hit me up at lazyfascist@gmail.com.

Cheers,

Cameron Pierce

CPSIA information can be obtained at www.ICGtesting.com
Printed in the USA
BVOW08n1943280815

415119BV00002B/45/P